Soulfully yours

Soulfully yours

MARITA BERRY

SOULFULLY YOURS

iUniverse books may be ordered through booksellers or by contacting:

iUniverse
1663 Liberty Drive
Bloomington, IN 47403
www.iuniverse.com
1-800-Authors (1-800-288-4677)

Because of the dynamic nature of the Internet, any web addresses or links contained in this book may have changed since publication and may no longer be valid. The views expressed in this work are solely those of the author and do not necessarily reflect the views of the publisher, and the publisher hereby disclaims any responsibility for them.

Any people depicted in stock imagery provided by Getty Images are models, and such images are being used for illustrative purposes only.
Certain stock imagery © Getty Images.

ISBN: 978-1-5320-9429-3 (sc)
ISBN: 978-1-6632-0469-1 (e)

Library of Congress Control Number: 2020912137

Print information available on the last page.

iUniverse rev. date: 07/30/2020

For all the hapless online daters of the world ... may you find truth and love in your cyber quest for lifelong companionship.

Acknowledgments

Usually, nothing great comes to pass without teamwork, and I am fortunate to have had a terrific team behind me. I owe my family a debt of gratitude for their unwavering encouragement and patience for an unashamed dreamer.

To my sister friends, you have my heartfelt thanks. It's been more than a pleasure to have known and loved you all these years. You have inspired me to write my stories.

Lastly, I want to thank my significant other, Arthur "Artie" Spencer, who believed in me even when I didn't believe in myself. He supported me unconditionally and always had my back, and for that I will be forever grateful. Now that he is in the glory of the Lord, I know he is peaceful, because here on earth he always did good and strived to be happy every day of his life. Rest in peace, my friend, until we meet again.

1

Toni Marie Summers eased her 1999 baby-blue Porsche Boxster into the parking lot of a twenty-story skyscraper tucked deep in the central business district of downtown Atlanta. She pulled into her reserved spot, parked, and pressed the button to turn off her CD of Miles Davis, noting how brilliant blue the winter sky looked. Winter. It was not her favorite time of year. Unlike farther south, Atlanta had four distinct seasons, and she liked the cold of winter the least. She enjoyed fall above the rest of the seasons of the year because of the beautiful colors of the leaves adorning the foothills of the nearby Blue Ridge Mountains. She shut down the car, smiling to herself in a moment of quiet reflection as she picked up her Louis Vuitton handbag and leather briefcase from the back seat, being careful not to cause a run in her black sheer stockings.

January 7 marked her thirty-fifth birthday, and the beautiful weather was quite fitting, at least in her view. In a sense, the day marked a milestone for her, what with it being almost five years to the month when she and her two girlfriends, Audrey Simmons and Lorna Stanley, pitched in together to start the public relations firm of Toni Summers and Associates. As the key financial backer, made possible through the life insurance payout she inherited from her biological parents on their death, Toni held 50 percent of the company and served as its CEO. The going had been tough only for a little while. The boon times of the mid-1990s meant there was plenty of work. The city was thriving. Venture capitalists and tech companies were flocking to America's jewel of the South, and Toni grabbed the opportunity and ran with it.

Now, five years later, the turn of the new century seemed to hold nothing but promise. The fake Y2K monster, otherwise known as the Millennium Bug, had mercifully failed to materialize and cause a global meltdown at the stroke of midnight on New Year's Eve, and yet for Toni the dawning of a new century seemed momentous in a way she didn't quite understand. She just knew that things in the universe were definitely conspiring to make waves in her otherwise orderly, controlled, and extraordinarily busy life.

Toni shook her head and sighed, her smile vanishing as the reality of her realm prodded her to make a conscious connection between her feelings of satisfaction and discontentment. Although things were going well in the company, not all was well with the world, her world, her own personal slice of life as a single woman who had soared to the top of her field. She lacked the male companionship most women wanted, that tender loving feeling of snuggling against a man in bed on an early morning. No sex. No talking. Just being. Just listening to the patter of a light rain on the window, the gray light of dawn giving the bedroom a soft, cozy ambience. She didn't need a man to make her whole, to complete her. She was too self-assured and confident in her own abilities for that, but, like most everyone else, she didn't like feeling lonely, and she wasn't sure what to do about it. She wasn't sure she even had time if she did know how to fill the black hole that had been with her for a very long time. She didn't want to hash over the bad stuff right before going up to her office to lose herself in her work.

"Get a grip, girl," she said as she got out of the car, purse in hand, and strode toward the glass doors of the lobby, her stiletto heels click-click-clicking on the sidewalk.

As she approached the front steps of the building, she noticed a tall, distinguished-looking guy, probably in his late fifties, gave her the once over. She knew she'd held her good looks, looks that had made her popular with men for all the wrong reasons. She couldn't stand it when men talked to her breasts instead of looking into her dark, almond-shaped eyes. At five-foot-six, she wasn't exactly petite, nor was she a stick like so many of the white women her age and in positions of power like hers, the ones who worried about getting fat when they looked downright anorexic. At 120 pounds, she had some meat on her, but not too much. She was happy with her body, her looks. An African American woman with a mocha complexion and straight, shoulder-length dark brown hair, she possessed an exotic appeal she knew was attractive to men. The problem was guys seemed to never look beyond the skin-deep to see what she had to offer from her heart.

Toni made her way into the lobby, passed through security, and headed to the elevators. People in the elevator all stared at the doors, not making eye contact with the other passengers in the car. That was fine with Toni. She suddenly felt pensive, discontent, and she didn't understand why she should feel that way on her birthday. Perhaps she felt the way she did because it *was* her birthday.

Although she tried to push them away, thoughts of her childhood flashed through her mind. She'd been too young to remember her biological parents. They were killed in a head-on collision when she was only nine months old. That one fateful event charted the course of her life thereafter, and all because some guy decided to drink and drive. Her maternal aunt took her in, but then she died when Toni was five years old, propelling her into the sometimes cruel and always lonely life in the foster system for the next seven years until she was taken in and later adopted by two loving people, both of whom were teachers. She finally had the family she'd always craved, including an older sister and brother to look up to.

Her adoptive parents instilled in her a desire to succeed, and she had done just that. In high school, she'd been a straight-A student, and she'd gone on to pursue her undergraduate and graduate studies on an academic scholarship to Clark Atlanta University, where she received an MBA in business administration. When she graduated, she got a job in consumer marketing. She learned the proverbial ropes, and she soon realized the glass ceiling truly did exist, especially for a woman of color. Starting her own business seemed to be the only way to get away from the constant, though often subtle, discrimination, the patronizing and condescending crap handed down from old white men in the executive suite.

The elevator doors opened, and everyone pushed out onto the fifteenth floor. Toni joined the well-dressed executives, admins, and other support staff as they all hurried to their respective offices. She'd almost arrived at her suite when she saw Scotty Walker, the head of security, coming toward her. He looked tight and buffed dressed in his navy-blue uniform, white shirt, and red tie.

Hot damn! For a forty-year-old his body is slamming, she thought, suppressing a smile at the realization she thought this almost every time she laid eyes on the man.

She reminded herself Scotty was once featured in *Atlanta Magazine* as one of the city's most eligible bachelors. In the next moment, he stopped in front of her. She didn't exactly have to crane her neck to look him in the eye. At six-two, he only had half a foot on her in height. His smooth milk-chocolate skin, hazel-brown eyes, and his sexy head of hair trimmed into a businesslike fade made him extremely striking. She smiled up at him, aware of the fragrance of his musk cologne. It was intoxicating, sending a tingling sensation throughout her entire body. Suddenly, Toni's face flushed and she hoped he didn't see it.

"Good morning, Miss Summers. Nice day we're having, isn't it? A shame to be cooped up in this here ivory tower." Grinning, he flashed his perfect white teeth. "And you look as beautiful as ever."

"Why, thank you, Scotty. Yes, it is a nice day out," she answered, making eye contact.

After a moment of awkward silence, she said she had to get going, that she had to get ready for an important teleconference slated to begin at nine. As she walked to her suite, she could feel his eyes burning a hole in her back. Toni thought she heard a low whistle, but chose to ignore it. After all, she wasn't the least bit interested in him.

Oh, who the hell am I kidding? He's so damn sexy!

Toni had a thing for men in uniforms. Two years earlier, she'd seen an ad in the *Atlanta Journal-Constitution* for the brand-new twenty-story art deco building. She inquired about office space for her growing company. Still half-empty, the building housed only a few tenants at that time. For Toni, moving up in style and space made perfect sense. In PR, image was everything. She'd met Scotty back then when she went to see about renting space in the building, and he'd been very flirtatious with her ever since. She found it enticing, but after not being in a committed relationship for four years, despite the pangs of occasional loneliness, Toni wanted to remain focused on her company. At least that's what she told herself.

Toni let herself into her suite and flipped on the lights in the reception area. Walking a short distance to the office kitchen, she opened the door, switched on the light, and paused before going in. Something was awry, and then it hit her, the usual aroma of coffee was missing. The microwave and coffee maker were all cleaned and still untouched from the night before.

Hmmm, that's odd. I thought I saw Alicia's car in the parking lot.

Her stomach grumbled, and she wished she'd eaten something before rushing to work. She made a beeline to the pantry and opened the cabinet. Alicia, the office manager, always kept it stocked with granola bars, single servings of cereals, coffee, herbal teas, cookies, and other treats. A basket of fresh fruit remained on the countertop. Good snacks were important to staff morale, especially when everyone was stressed out on deadline. Not finding anything appetizing, Toni opened the refrigerator and found bottles of sparkling water, lemons, and assorted juices. She took a bottle of sparkling water and grabbed an apple from the basket before continuing down the hall to her office.

On the way, she noticed Lorna and Audrey's offices were empty. Toni glanced at her watch. It was a bit before eight-thirty, and the conference call was scheduled for nine o'clock.

"Where is everyone?" she wondered. "Traffic in the loop wasn't that bad."

Toni opened the door to her corner office and turned on the lights, feeling the surge of self-satisfaction she always felt whenever she entered her inner sanctum. Two mahogany studded leather couches sat on each side of the room, and the antique desk by the window with a high-back mahogany matching chair added punch to the neutral walls and hardwood flooring.

A built-in bookcase spanned the wall opposite the expansive windows. The shelves were home to books by some of her favorite authors, and assorted family mementos. There was a photograph of herself as an infant, wrapped in a soft pink blanket, held by her biological mother. That particular photograph ranked as one of her most valued possessions. On the walls were additional pictures of her biological parents, some of her adoptive parents, both her degrees, and tastefully done modern art.

Placing her briefcase on the desk, she partially opened the horizontal blinds to let some sunshine inside. She paused, taking in the magnificent view of Atlanta's cityscape. She also had a stunning view of the city from her luxury high-rise condo in the chic section of Buckhead, one of many suburbs that continued to spew urban sprawl ever outward into the countryside. Aesthetics were important to her, which was why the views played a big part in her choice of locations for her home and office. Toni sat down at her desk, reached into the bottom side drawer, and extracted the file folders she needed for the teleconference. She felt relieved she had worked late the night before updating the client's records and returning phone calls while her associates were out in the field interviewing new clients.

Toni, Audrey, and Lorna had met in their freshmen year at Clark Atlanta University. At first, it was Toni and Audrey who were dorm mates, while Lorna stayed in the room across from theirs. Since Lorna's roommate never showed up, she spent most nights alone. By the end of their first semester, Lorna's personal belongings were stuffed in Toni and Audrey's already overcrowded room. The following semester, they petitioned the dean of housing for a larger room so they could all live together.

Separately, each one brought something special to the company. Lorna was in charge of the media and press releases while Toni and Audrey divided their time focusing on marketing, advertising, and sales. Lorna was light-skinned with finely carved features, shoulder-length curly black hair, and gray eyes. As the girls later found out, Lorna's mother was black, and her father was white. At five-seven, she was just an inch or so taller than Toni, and they both weighed about the same at just south of 120. With her exotic beauty, Lorna had done a little modeling in her senior year of high school, and she could've gone on to the big time, in Toni's estimation. But, true to her word, she followed through on the promise she made to her parents that she would go to college, get a degree, and land a real job when she graduated. Although she was friendly and easygoing, there were times when Lorna seemed very weak when it came to men. And, like many beautiful women, most men only wanted to use her as a trophy on their arms, or as a sex toy in bed.

Basically, down-to-earth in terms of personality, Audrey sometimes came off as aggressive to her coworkers. Well cultured, she had traveled to several African and European countries in her lifetime. Nicknamed "Red" because of her dyed red hair, she was five feet, five inches tall and had a scatter of freckles across her caramel-toned nose and cheeks. She had a certain allure that was irresistible to men, too.

No matter how much drama they went through, they dealt with it together and bonded like sisters. This was especially important to Toni since she was the one who was adopted. Family was important to her, almost as much as business, power, and success in a male-dominated profession. Indeed, most professions remained male-dominated, even in the year 2000, despite the efforts of women to achieve equality with men. It was tough to be a woman in the C-level suite, and even tougher for a woman of color. Toni wasn't bitter about it, though she disliked the way most women were treated in the workplace. She saw no point in getting overly worked up about something she had no power to change, except in her own company.

Feeling slightly annoyed her key staff were late for work, she gathered the files she needed for the teleconference. She couldn't afford to blow this account. It was for a large accounting firm in Chicago that wanted to add a satellite location in the downtown Atlanta area. They were referred to Toni by a satisfied client, and she wanted to be certain they made a good presentation. She believed Alicia may have dashed out across the street to the pharmacy, as she often did, to fill her mother's prescription. It was odd she wasn't at her desk, and that nobody else seemed to be either. Noticing the message light on her phone blinking, she decided the messages would have to wait. Toni retrieved a few legal pads and pens and walked down the hall with her files.

She opened the door to the conference room …

"Surprise!"

Alicia, Lorna, Audrey, Alicia, several of the admins, and a handful of clients all were wearing party hats, and the room was decorated in her favorite colors of purple and lavender. A happy birthday banner stretched across the width of the windows. Helium-filled colored balloons floated overhead, and arrangements of flowers, cake plates, and utensils had been placed on the conference table next to a frosted sheet cake with the message *Happy Birthday, Toni*. Platters of bite-sized breakfast sandwiches, containers of orange juice, coffee cups, and a coffee urn perched on a side table. On the credenza by the window were various gift bags and wrapped boxes.

"Happy birthday, girl!" Audrey and Lorna screamed.

They quickly came forward and hugged her.

"Thank you, guys, so much!" Toni said, hugging them back. "I can't believe all of this is for me?" Her voice cracked as she tried to hold back the tears. "No wonder no one was in their offices and I didn't smell coffee brewing."

"You deserve it boss," Alicia said.

"You know I don't like surprises," Toni said, "but I like this one."

In all the excitement, she'd momentarily forgotten about the conference call. Suddenly, she was all business. "Hey, guys! What about the conference call?"

"Oh," Alicia said. "We rescheduled it. Pushed it back to ten."

"Okay," Toni said, feeling annoyed and touched at the same time.

"Come on now, tell the truth. You weren't really surprised, were you?" Audrey asked, flipping a strand of her dreadlocked hair behind her ear. She had the rest of it pinned up in a fashionable bun. If she didn't pin it up, the longest of the dreads reached the middle of her back. Audrey had always worn her hair natural since her early college days. She said she was born without chemicals in her hair and she was going to die that way. The kelly green pantsuit and mint blouse she wore went well with her fiery red hair.

"No. Really, I didn't have a clue. You all did a good job keeping this from me," Toni said.

"Honestly, this was all Alicia's idea," Lorna said.

Toni relied a great deal on Alicia as the office manager. Alicia stood just about five feet tall. She had a young girl's body and all the right curves, although she swore she never exercised a day in her life. Her boyish haircut matched her tawny complexion. At only twenty-five, she was single with no children. She often said her main goal in life was to one day become a top publicist. She managed the office single-handedly and kept the ladies' handiwork in tip-top order. She was initially hired as a temporary office worker, but after she proved to be so efficient, energetic, and dependable, they all agreed to hire her permanently.

"You know for an old hag, you look pretty good for thirty-five," Audrey laughed, giving her another hug.

"Thanks, Red. But before you go calling somebody an old hag, don't forget you're a year older than me," Toni said.

"Oh, yeah, I forgot," Audrey smiled, and went to sit back at the table.

Lorna was next. She was dressed in an expensive navy-blue pantsuit, and the pearl necklace set off the color. Her short hair looked like a curly mop on top of her head. Up close, Toni noticed her puffy face and watery eyes.

"I can't believe in another few years we're all going to be forty. It seems like yesterday when we first met in college. I don't know where the time went," she said, giving Toni a quick hug.

"I can't believe it either, sweetie, but it's all good. We're just like fine wine getting better with age." Toni leaned close and whispered, "Are you okay?"

"I'm fine. It's my allergies acting up again," Lorna said.

The others in the room approached Toni and hugged her, too. Toni did her best to maintain her composure. Then everyone congregated around the cake and sang happy birthday to her. She closed her eyes, made a wish, and blew out the candles.

"Hey, Toni, what did you wish for?" Lorna asked.

"Yeah, tell us!" the others chimed in.

Toni wagged her finger at them and said, "If I tell you, then my wish won't come true! Everybody knows that."

"I bet I know what you wished for!" Audrey giggled.

Toni shot a glance at her in an attempt to shut her up. Audrey just shook her head and placed her finger over her lips.

Later that evening, Toni leaned back in the booth at Pittypat's Porch, one of her favorite restaurants in the city. Not being a heavy drinker, she already felt the effects of the champagne she, Audrey, and Lorna were imbibing in celebration of landing the new account earlier in the day. Of course, they were celebrating their monthly Friday evening outings as well as Toni's birthday. Toni felt at ease, totally at ease, in fact, and she didn't mind letting her hair down.

"*Soooo,* Toni, now that you're thirty-five, aren't you feeling a wee bit lonely? You know the older you get the harder it is to meet men," Audrey said. "Not that it seems to bother you any."

Toni placed her fork on her plate, took another sip of champagne, and dismissively waved her free hand as if she was shooing away a pesky fly.

"You're not gonna start in with that again, are you? I mean … come on! It's getting old already."

"Why is it you get upset every time I talk about your love life? You know as well as I do you wished for a man when you blew out your birthday candles."

Toni flinched, almost as if she'd received a mild shock. She knew Audrey didn't mean to hurt her feelings, but she had anyway. And on her birthday, no less.

"Tonight, I just want to celebrate my birthday with my best girlfriends and live in the moment. I'm content being single. You know I haven't been in a serious relationship in four years, and, truth be told, I frankly haven't missed it much. I think I'd miss chocolate more if it went away for the duration."

"Yeah, right! That's such a crock. You tellin' me you haven't gotten any in four dang years? Girl, you ain't foolin' no one," Lorna said, getting a little street on Toni. "Nobody can go bone dry for that long. Except maybe you. Might explain why you sometimes strut around with a broomstick stuck up where the sun don't shine."

Toni sighed, shook her head. How long had it been since she'd been intimate with a man? Too long, at least in her book. She'd learned long ago how to play the sex game. Men made it easy. Men didn't seem to want relationships, at least not real relationships, more than they wanted sex. Therefore, it was easy to scratch the itch in any upscale bar in the city. Bat her eyes, wear a low-cut blouse to show off plenty of cleavage, and act like a stupid chick on the prowl for some fun. Worked every time. And then, like a rain in the desert, she'd romp in a field of wildflowers until the joy evaporated into hot thin air, and she'd keep on keeping on until she needed to find a new oasis to satisfy her occasional thirsts.

"You know how it is, Lorna, so lighten up, okay? Don't ruin my birthday. Like I said. Let's live in the moment and forget about men."

Lorna laughed, then turned to Audrey, and said, "Yeah, Miss Audrey. Besides, what about your love life? I haven't heard you mention going on any dates lately. You ask me it seems like you live the life of a nun. Or even worse, if that was ever possible."

"Well, as a matter of fact, I do have a date tomorrow night, and it's with someone I met online. So there. Shows how much you *don't* know."

"On the Internet?" Lorna asked, raising an eyebrow. "You met your date online?"

Audrey nodded vigorously. "Yeah, online. Get with the program, girl! It's a new century! Internet dating is bigtime these days. What's the matter? You living in a damned cave or somthin'?"

"Internet dating always seems creepy to me," Lorna said. "You never know if the guy you're gonna meet is some sort of psycho dude or something. Hell, he could come off like a movie star in his fake internet profile when in fact he's just a plain old nutjob who's ready to do you no good whatsoever."

"Or … he could be a total *perv*," Toni said. "You ever think about that?"

"They get totally screened, you guys," Audrey said. She leaned forward over the table. Toni noted that Audrey seemed to be staring right at her with a hidden point in mind. It was cool. She'd known Audrey long enough to figure out when she had something snugged up under her sleeve.

"Did you know the first online dating site launched only six years ago?"

Toni shook her head, as did Lorna.

"No kidding? For real?" Toni asked, her interest fanned. "Tell me more."

"Yeah, the first dating site ever was called kiss.com. Then match.com launched in 1995. Believe it or not, online dating sites were the whole big new rage just a few years ago. By 1996 there were sixteen online dating sites hawking their wares to lonely singles. Can you believe that? Now that's a whole bunch of horny singles!"

"Amazing," Toni said.

"What? Horny singles? Nothin' amazing about that," Lorna said.

"Shut up, girl!" Toni said, taking another sip of her champagne, emptying her glass, and refilling it. She emptied the bottle in the process.

"Yeah, and now it's all eharmony.com this and eharmony.com that," Lorna said. "I get sick of hearing the ads."

"The site just launched in August," Audrey said, sounding to Toni almost like she expected them all to know the straight skinny on online dating sites. "That's why you keep hearing their ads on the radio and seeing them on TV."

"Uh-huh," Toni said. "I'd rather just leave this all be for now, okay?

Like I said. Let's forget about men for now. They're so not worth the bother. Let's not ruin a great day and a better night with scat talk on the little peckers in the neighborhood."

"Oh, no," Lorna said. "Our girl's not getting off that easy. How long have you known him?" she asked Audrey. "And, by the way, what's his name and what does he do?"

"If you must know, we've been exchanging emails for a few weeks now," Audrey said. "That's how it usually goes. And his name is David, he's a junior partner for a family law firm."

Lorna scoffed. "And you believe that? Really? The guy probably looks nothing like his photo. He probably Photoshopped the whole thing to make him look sexy when he's probably as fat as a watermelon and as bald as a cue ball. And he's probably unemployed to boot!"

Toni, her interest in the online business side of the internet still fanned, asked how Audrey knew so much about the early history of online dating sites. Audrey laughed and told her she'd done her homework out of a sense of self-preservation.

"You can do all you want," Lorna said, "but in the end, you're still meeting up with someone who could be a serial killer."

"No shit, Sherlock," Toni said. She laughed, ran her hand through her hair, and held up the empty bottle of champagne, suddenly not wanting to go back to her condo in Buckhead. "You guys up for another?"

Audrey groaned and shook her head no.

Toni noticed Audrey looked like she wanted to get going. "Okay. Okay, I get it." She looked at her watch. "I know we really should pack it in. And we will! Just one more question. Where are you going to meet him?"

"I figured we'd meet at the sports bar over on Peachtree Street, where there'll be lots of people."

Toni felt relieved. She knew Audrey could take care of herself, but even the most capable woman might fall short if confronted with a psycho killer.

"Well, then," Toni said, "you best watch your ass, okay?"

"You got it, sister!" Audrey said.

Audrey took another big sip of her champagne, wiped her mouth with the back of her right hand, and burped. Everyone laughed. Audrey set her glass down and said, "I think I can trust David. After all, I found him on Soulfully Yours."

"Soulfully who?" Lorna asked.

"Soulfully Yours," Audrey said. "They're supposedly the hottest hookup site for African Americans in the entire metro Atlanta area."

That got Toni's interest. "Oh, really?"

"Yeah. Really!" Audrey said. "If they can't hook you up, nobody can."

Toni paused for a moment. She was definitely feeling the effects of the champagne now. It had been a long time since she'd drunk so much, and she didn't like the feeling of not being in control. "I may have lots to offer, but right now the store is closed."

"To hell with you two heifers. I'm still going on my date," Audrey said.

Just then, the waiter appeared with a small cake with a lit number thirty-five candle on top.

Toni placed her hand on her heart and smiled. "For me?"

"Of course! You know we always end the night with something sweet," Lorna said.

They sang happy birthday to her again, and Toni made another wish before leaning forward and blowing out the candles.

"You know what I wished for this time ladies?"

"Don't have a clue," Lorna said.

"I thank God for having two wonderful friends. I love you guys so much."

As Toni finished off the last of the champagne in her glass, she once again acknowledged that Audrey and Lorna were the rocks in her life, a collective island of female power that enabled her to keep moving forward even when she felt totally alone and isolated. She smiled at Audrey and said, "Let's call it a night, girls! I think I've had a bit too much bubbly."

"You and me both," Lorna said.

A little wobbly on her feet, Toni got up and slid into her jacket. A few moments later, she and her friends were outside on the sidewalk in front of the restaurant. "You guys take care," she said, her words slightly slurred.

"Back at ya birthday girl!" Audrey said.

"Ditto!" Lorna said.

Both ladies then turned and headed in the opposite direction after their group hug. Toni watched them go, the dull glow of alcohol already fading into the headache she knew was on its way in a hurry. As she walked to her car, she thought about Audrey and her upcoming date with David.

13

Could she be onto something? Toni wondered.

For a moment, she pictured herself in the arms with a man right out of a romance novel, and she suddenly felt embarrassed. Yet, as she unlocked her Porsche, got in, and revved the engine, she couldn't help but smile at the warm sensation she began to feel when she thought of how wonderful it would be to find that special someone, a man with intellect, sensitivity, passion, and money. Lots of money.

"Where have you been all my life?" she said with a laugh. "Nowhere near me, that's for sure."

Toni shook her head as she pulled out of the parking spot and headed home. She vowed to put thoughts of men out of her mind, but she knew she would never be able to do that.

Change is coming, she thought, *and there's nothing you can do about it.*

2

Toni sat up in bed, pushing her tousled hair behind her ears and glancing toward the expansive sliding glass doors that led from her bedroom to the balcony. She could see the sun was about to rise because the condo faced east, affording her the privilege of watching the orange orb edge above the Atlanta skyline. A habitual early riser, she'd chosen the condo for the view, and because she knew she'd awaken to see the spectacular sunrises more than most people who spent their literal and figurative lives in bed with their eyes closed and their minds on snooze. She groaned. Her head throbbed from having one too many glasses of champagne the night before.

You really are an idiot sometimes, she thought.

Yawning, she stretched as she got out of bed and headed into the bathroom to do her usual morning business, acknowledging she'd treated herself to a rare night out with her best friends. Sure, the three of them always got together once every month to let their hair down, as it were, but somehow the previous evening was different. It had been a nice way to end her birthday, and the entire day had been a victory since she and the team had landed that big client from Chicago. Yet, Audrey's talk about online dating stuck with her. The idea of using the internet to find a soul mate seemed ludicrous to Toni, but it was a new century. The internet had already gone way beyond AOL.com and the famous dial-up male robotic voice of "you've got mail!" Was Audrey really crazy, or was she onto something that could possibly change her life for the better? Audrey's words about men from the night before came back to her.

The older a woman gets, the harder it becomes to find a man.

After nearly four years of hardly dating on a serious level, Toni was tired of the loneliness. She didn't even get much sexual pleasure from the one-night stands she sometimes initiated in her frequent dark hours of intense emotional and physical need. In a way, all the success she'd achieved didn't seem worth it if she didn't have someone to share it with. Hell, she didn't even have a cat. And she didn't want one either. But, as she brushed her teeth, she admitted she did want a man, and not just for sex. Not just for the physical release that could send her to the stars in the hands of the right lover. She wanted something more, something substantial, something that could last a lifetime with just a dash of luck and a pinch of sincerity.

Aware that she was putting herself in a bad mood with all the negative self-talk, she made the conscious effort to push the unpleasant thoughts and feelings away. Still, she wondered what it was about men that made them so attractive and yet so perpetually stupid. She also wondered what it was about women that seemed to point them always on the path to relationships that ended up being bad car wrecks. Sadly, some of the men she met either wanted to be taken care of, or else become friends with sex benefits, while others didn't know what they wanted. She often wondered if her expectations were too high, but she didn't think so. In fact, she thought she'd lowered her expectations to the point where she no longer thought dating netted a decent return on investment. The return of investment on the dating scene just didn't cut it in her book, and she didn't believe it had much to do with her numbers in the male accounting ledger.

She finished brushing her teeth and ventured into her walk-in closet to get dressed. Although it was a Saturday, she wasn't taking the day off. She intended to put in at least a half day's work in her home office. She got a lot done at home because there was nobody around to interrupt her. The normalcy of her morning routine was comforting in a way, but that nagging sense of discontentment had surfaced so recently continued to nudge at the fringes of her consciousness.

Toni had promised herself by the time she was thirty she would be successful in public relations, financially independent, and at least married.

Children were another factor in her long-term thinking. She liked babies. She thought they were cute. She wasn't sure she would be a great mom, though, and so the dire ticking of a woman's biological clock remained a slight tick, tick, tick far in the background of her conscious thinking. She did, however, acknowledge time was running out if she changed her mind and decided to take the baby plunge … if she met the right man.

The growth of her business had allowed her to fulfill some of her lifelong goals. First and foremost, she had wanted a home that was all hers. Being a foster kid left a lasting impression on her. Stability, predictability, and security were all super important to Toni. So, when her PR firm really took off and she was able to purchase her luxury condo, it really meant something to her. The closing day represented a major milestone moment for her.

The condo was a large spacious two-bedroom residence with a washer and dryer, huge living room with a fireplace, kitchen, dining room area, two baths, and a private balcony with a lovely view of downtown. She loved lying in her four-poster bed with red and beige linens. A natural beige fiber rug added a contrast of color to the hardwood flooring. Abstract paintings, a chaise lounge, a nightstand with lamp, a chandelier, and a wardrobe filled with designer clothes, shoes, and bags were all essential elements of any bedroom, at least in her humble view.

As far as the living room was concerned, Toni had pulled out all the stops. The room featured built-in floor-to-ceiling bookcases stacked with first editions from some of the nation's more famous African-American authors, African sculptures, modern art, and a cognac-colored couch with accent pillows. The leopard throw did look a bit garish. Lorna hated it.

"Girl! What you doing with a leopard motif in such a classy place?" Lorna had asked. "You'd think you grew up in a doublewide."

"I dunno," Toni had said. "I kinda like it. Besides, honey, I live here. You don't."

Toni finished getting dressed and went to the kitchen, poured a glass of water, and gulped down two aspirins. Then she turned on the coffeemaker. Walking back through the living room, she hesitated at the door of her second bedroom, which she had converted into her home office. An oak desk with a computer, a fax machine, and an ergonomic chair were set up in front of the window. A nice geometric black and white area rug, a bookcase, and a series of framed black-and-white pictures provided a slightly sterile and yet comfortable ambiance. The photos, most of them landscapes devoid of people, were hers. Many had been taken on her numerous solo vacations to the British Virgin Islands. On the desk were a stack of client files she had brought home to update before the next meeting.

She hurried back into the kitchen and made her coffee. As she stirred in the cream and sugar, she thought again about Audrey. Could it really be that easy to find a man who didn't end up being a class-A jerk? Could the power of the internet do all the screening for her? Long before she found herself sitting across the table from a guy who was about as compatible with her as a cat was with a dead mouse? The relationship in that case would only benefit the cat. It wasn't such a great thing for the mouse. Why was it that so many relationships left her feeling like the mouse, and not the cat?

Toni took another sip of her coffee, sighed, and gazed out the kitchen window. The sun was higher now. The orange hue illuminated the city skyline, setting the skyscrapers off against a brilliant blue sky. The January air was particularly crisp. She could tell just by looking. She didn't need to go outside on her balcony. On a whim, she went into her home office, sat down at the desk, and turned on her computer. When the machine was ready for use, she keyed Soulfully Yours into her search engine, and up popped the website. She browsed through some of the testimonials and saw several couples, some interracial, which encouraged Toni. Audrey had said the site was geared toward African Americans, particularly men and women on the upper end of the financial scale. She wondered why she was wasting her time, but, deep down inside, she knew she was more than just curious about this online dating option. True, the first site had come online just six years earlier, but internet hookups seemed to be the way of the future at the dawn of the new millennium. She figured she owed it to herself to at least scope the scene out.

You mean to tell me all these people met here on this site? This looks too good to be true.

She scrolled through several profiles of men she found interesting. She read everything, getting lost in the fantasy of it, and then she stopped cold.

I don't know where to begin. Do I actually have to tell them everything about me in order to pique their interest?

Toni was well aware of her stubborn streak, that she always finished what she started. She decided to create an online profile almost to prove to Audrey she had the guts to put herself back out on the meat market. Her hands shaking, in part from the hangover and in part from fear, she typed in her name and email address. Suddenly, her heartrate increased. Sweat trickled down her spine and moistened her underarms.

What are you doing? This whole scene isn't right for you! Who do you think you're kidding anyway?

Toni panicked and logged out before starting an account. She didn't know if she was ready to start dating again just yet. Instead, she checked her email, and decided she'd wait to ask Audrey for more information on Monday. A call came in, but she let the answering machine take it, although she did hover to find out the caller was Lorna. Toni almost picked up the receiver, but she thought better of it.

I'll call her later.

Toni arrived at work on Monday morning feeling perky and refreshed with her updated client folders in tow. She had just sat down at her desk and opened her scheduling account when her office door opened. Toni looked up.

"Hey, Toni, got a minute?"

It was Audrey with her hands full of DVDs, and she seemed excited.

"Sure, Red. What's up?"

Toni saved the schedule she was working on as Audrey came in and closed the door.

"What do you have there?" she asked.

"I stopped by the video store after my date this weekend, and I picked up some of my favorite movies. Wanna see 'em?"

"Sure. Let's see what you have."

Audrey spread them across her desk.

"Hmmm." Toni plucked through them. "*Love Story. An Affair to Remember. Mahogany.* Audrey, these are all movies about love."

"Yeah. But they're different kinds of love—romantic love, friendship love, and unconditional love. I was in the mood for a love marathon this weekend."

Audrey sat down in one of the chairs across from Toni's desk.

"I gather you had a nice time with this guy. What's his name, by the way?"

"We had a great first date! And his name is David. Like I told you."

Toni sighed. "Yeah. Right. I forgot. So, anyway, you guys hit it off?"

"We sure did! It was awesome," Audrey said. "We met at the sports bar as planned. It felt as though we'd known each other for years. Throughout the whole meal, he kept looking at me with this twinkle in his eyes. I think there was a physical attraction between us. But I didn't want to look desperate, so I begrudgingly kept looking down at my plate."

"No way," Toni said, laughing.

"Yes. Way. When we finished dinner, it was still early and he wanted to hang out some more, but he had no ideas about where to go, which I thought was a little weird. I asked him if he was new in town, and he said he's been working so hard he didn't know much about all the cool places to hang out. I figured we could go dancing. I took him over to that dance club on Piedmont. A friend of mine was cocktailing there, and I knew at least a handful of her friends would be there, so I wouldn't have to be alone with him if things got uncomfortable."

Toni leaned back in her chair, steepled her fingers, and smiled at her friend. Audrey seemed to literally glow. Her eyes sparkled. Her voice contained elements of joy, or something that Toni hadn't heard for a good long while.

"About ten minutes after we arrived, Barbara came over and I introduced them, and then she offered us a drink on the house."

Toni listened to her friend describe the rest of her date with David. As she listened, she began to feel jealous, and that surprised her. She knew she should be happy for Audrey, and she was. It was just she also felt envious, and lonely.

"When it was time to go home, he took me back to get my car, and then we went our separate ways. He's a fantastic tongue kisser, too!" Audrey said.

"You mean you actually swapped spit on your first date?" Toni leaned forward, put her palms flat on the desk in front of her. "Seriously?"

"Where you been, girl? Under a rock or something? People do more than just tongue kiss on their first dates nowadays. You should know that."

"Yeah, but that's gross. You should at least get to know him a little better."

Audrey pushed the DVD's closer to Toni. "Girl, please! Why don't you take these home tonight? It might get you in the right mood."

Toni eyeballed them. "I would love to share in your love marathon, but there's no way I have time to look at these, especially tonight. I have three meetings scheduled today, so there's no telling what time I'll be getting home."

Audrey sighed.

"As a matter of fact," Toni said. "I've been thinking about what we discussed on Friday. You know … about signing up for that dating service. I actually checked out the Soulfully Yours website."

"Really?" Audrey said. "Frankly, I'm surprised."

"I'm surprised too," Toni said. "I guess you really got to me. Or maybe it's because I just turned thirty-five and realized I have no one to share things with. It feels almost like what the hell is the point of my working so damned hard just to go home, sleep, and get up and do it all over again the next day."

"I hear you," Audrey said. "Boy, do I ever hear you! You know what?"

"What?"

"Alicia has tried the site too," Audrey said, shooting Toni a grin. "So, you're not the only one to be poking around to see how green the grass is."

"No! Get out of here! You mean Alicia is looking for a man, too? I guess everyone's biological clock is ticking. Loneliness can be a real mother."

Toni suddenly felt very sad. She hated feeling vulnerable, open, and exposed to the barbs of the world, to the foibles and imperfections of humanity. She'd known Audrey since college, but how well did she really know her friend? How well did anyone really know anyone else? She got up from her chair and walked to the windows, her back to her friend.

"Yeah, I know. That's the reason why I started dating again. I'm sick and tired of going home to four walls and a fat goldfish," Audrey said.

Toni turned to face her friend. "You still got that fish? Thought it died months ago."

Audrey laughed. "Nope. Little bugger likes his little watery world. Or at least I guess he does. Anyways, he's still kickin'. Bless his heart!"

Toni sat down again. She suddenly made a decision based on Audrey's dating adventure. "I need you to tell me, step by step, what you did, so I'll know what to expect if I actually open an account."

Audrey did just that. The procedure sounded oddly like mounting an aggressive PR campaign, and when she said as much to Audrey her friend slapped both hands on her knees and laughed out loud.

"What do you think dating is? It's all about marketing. It's all about image. It's all about doing everything you can do to attract the fly to the fly paper. Once the fly lands, he's all yours 'cause he ain't getting away."

"That's sick," Toni said, her stomach sinking. The prospect of packaging herself like a pound of ground beef did nothing to push her on to making a decision she hoped, if all went well, it would change her life for the better. Still, nothing ventured, nothing gained.

The next couple of weeks were a bit chaotic for Toni between her demanding work schedule, and waiting for the results from the dating website. She had set up a new email address as Audrey had suggested, and filled in her profile truthfully. She listed her age, occupation, said she had no children, and uploaded two recent pictures of herself, a closeup and a full-body view. She indicated she wanted to meet a friend for dating only, nothing serious. The ideal candidate would be at least six feet tall, between forty and forty-five years of age, have the fear of God, financially stable, disease and recreational drug free, a nonsmoker, a social drinker, a man who loved his mother, and, most importantly, he would have to have a terrific sense of humor. Toni had spent enough of her early years in tears. She wanted to spend the rest of her life with a man who could make her laugh, even in the hard times.

Toni had returned home by nine o'clock one evening, and she went straight to her computer to sign on to the *Soulfully Yours* site. Chewing nervously on her lower lip, her fingers hovered over the keys. Then she signed on. Her profile came up stating she had four new hits. She'd gotten plenty of weird ones since she'd posted her profile in January. Now it was Mid-February and she still hadn't gone on a date. She tried to fight her frustration, but had been failing at it lately. She was losing hope, despite Audrey's encouragement. Seeing the four hits bolstered Toni's mood. She clicked on the first profile.

"What's this, a joke? I never said I was looking for a woman. I guess

some people will try anything to get a date. Sorry, sweetie not interested."
She deleted the woman's profile.

The next one was a Caucasian male. "You're cute, but no thanks, Bob.
I'm not ready to date outside of my race." She deleted that one too. She
realized she should keep an open mind about interracial dating. A man was
a man, after all, but she felt comfortable enough within herself to admit
she just didn't want the extra baggage that typically came with a salt-and-
pepper relationship. Finding the right mate was hard enough, evidently,
and she didn't want to complicate matters.

The third profile didn't have a picture with it. She remembered Audrey
saying if the profile didn't have a picture, it wasn't worth following-up on.
She deleted that one also.

By the time she came to the fourth profile, she was beginning to feel
a little disappointed. In the last week or two, she had begun to doubt
whether internet dating would work out for her. So many mismatched
hits. The site was supposed to be set up to make matches made in heaven,
but thus far it seemed like it was set up to just make her feel even more
lonely. Sighing, she clicked on the last profile, and her eyes widened at two
pictures of a tall, muscular man with a light brown complexion, an angular
face, and piercing dark brown eyes. His head was cue-ball bald, giving him
a slightly military look. In the closeup view, she was immediately drawn to
his handsome smile. He wore a white unbuttoned shirt with a matching
blazer that accentuated his pleasant facial features. The full view was a
shot of him standing poolside in tasteful black swim trunks. A partially
buttoned shirt in a Hawaiian pattern showcased his six-pack abs. Clearly,
the man was no stranger at the gym.

Her interest piqued, she scrolled through his profile, noting his name
was Donovan Tate and that they had similar values. He worked as a
computer specialist and didn't smoke. His stats listed him as age forty,
six foot one, and 210 pounds. Under his personality, he portrayed himself
as being ambitious, laidback, and easygoing. He said although he was
intensely private, he did have a sense of humor. He believed in God as a
higher power and was involved in community activism. In the brief email
he included with his post to her, he answered her question about whether
he loved his mom or not. She'd put that in her sorting criteria because
she knew from experience a man who didn't get along with his family,

especially his mom, would likely be trouble in the end. Donovan answered her question without apparently thinking anything of it. His mom was deceased, but he stressed he loved and missed her dearly.

"Okay, I think I'm going to pursue this one," Toni said with a smile.

She shut down the computer and went to get some much-needed sleep. As she drifted off, she pictured Donovan Tate in her mind's eye.

Are you the man for me? she wondered.

3

Toni arrived early at the office the next day with her mind in a whirl over numerous business matters. Yet, as she rode the elevator up to the fifteenth floor, she thought of Donovan Tate … the gorgeous specimen of a man who just might make an entrance in her life, if she let him. She'd been well aware that Lorna did not approve of internet dating. She said the whole thing as nothing but a sham, and no good could come of it. Toni wondered what Lorna would say when she told her about Donovan, and she intended to set up a meet-and-greet with him.

"If God wants you to find your soul mate, he'll set it up. Just like he did with me and Charles. See how it all worked out, Charles and I are now living together. You don't need a computer to find love. You just need faith," Lorna had said during one of their heated conversations. Another time she said, "See! You haven't been on a single date yet and it's been more than a month. Closer to two. Why don't you just give it up?"

Audrey, on the other hand, fully supported Toni's half-hearted efforts to find love in cyberspace. After all, she'd found David. She and David had been going strong for quite some time, and it looked to Toni like the relationship stood a decent chance of surviving the first real fight. If a relationship could endure Round 1, then it probably could endure Round 2, and all the rest of the rounds that would inevitably follow over time, if the glue between them continued to hold.

The day got off to a fast start as Toni presided over several back-to-back meetings. As the most recent one wound up, she looked at her watch, realized she'd skipped lunch. She glanced across the conference table at Audrey. Alicia and Lorna had just left, as had the rest of the marketing crew.

"I'm a little bit worried about Lorna," Audrey said, stretching her arms out in front of her and cracking her knuckles.

"Why would you say that?"

"She's been really moody ever since she and Charles moved in together. Haven't you noticed?"

"Well, to tell you the truth, I've been so busy lately I haven't noticed much of anything."

"Yeah, well, whenever you speak to her, she seems far off in another world. And then she gets to be quite the bitch for no apparent reason. You know we've known each other long enough to tell when something is wrong with one of us. Hell, we even finish each other's sentences. I'm tellin' you, Lorna is hiding something. Or whatever. I've asked her about what's wrong, but she says everything's fine."

Truth be told, Toni had noticed a change in Lorna. And that change correlated to Charles moving in with her. "Okay," Toni said. "I'll give her a call tonight. See if she'll open up to me."

And Toni did call her friend. She did so on the pretext of seeing whether Lorna wanted to do a girl's night on Friday—dinner and a show at one of their favorite comedy clubs.

"Thanks, Toni, but I'm gonna have to take a rain check on that."

"Come on, it'll be good for us to get out. Maybe you need a good laugh."

"Charles and I already have plans for Friday night."

"Oh," Toni said. "Uh, well … I'm sure he wouldn't mind if you canceled to have a night out with the girls."

"Don't count on it," Lorna said.

Was that despair Toni heard in Lorna's voice? She thought about it for a brief moment, and then pushed the thought away.

"Anyway," Lorna continued, "it's not worth the hassle of changing plans in midstream at this point. You understand how it is."

"Not sure if I do," Toni said. "Is everything okay between you and Charles? I mean … I know you've known him since college, but even back then he seemed like a jerk. Ever since you started hanging out with him again, Audrey and I have both noticed you've been avoiding us lately."

"Listen, Toni. Thanks to you and Audrey for your concern. But as you ladies already told me, we're all grown women and we make our own choices, so please respect mine."

"Okay," Toni said, surprised at Lorna's tone. "I hear you. Sorry. Didn't mean to intrude."

"No problem," Lorna said. After a brief pause, she said, "Hey, glad you called because I need to take care of some personal business. I won't be in next week."

"What personal business?"

"I'd rather not say right now, if that's okay with you," Lorna said.

Confusion distracted Toni. Finally, she said, "Okay, Lorna. If there's anything I can do, please keep me—"

"I gonna run. Charles just came home," she said and the line went dead.

Toni hung up and immediately called Audrey. When Audrey picked up, Toni told her that the conversation with Lorna about Charles had not gone well, and that Lorna was taking the following week off work.

"What? She wants to take the whole damn week off with such short notice? Toni,

we have enough work to do without having to pick up her slack."

"I know, but what can we do? The choice is hers. I'm sure if it were you or me,

we would want the other person to pitch in. Alicia will be happy to step in and help out with her accounts. Besides, it will give her a chance to get some on-hands experience."

"I guess you're right. But like I told you. Something is going on with her, and you need to find out what it is. Maybe you should invite her to lunch or something. I think she might be more comfortable talking to you one-on-one."

"I'm not so sure about that. I invited her to go with me this Friday night to the comedy club, but she passed."

"Weird," Audrey said. "David and I would love to join you, if you like."

"Let me think on that. You know, I found a guy on Soulfully who looks interesting. Maybe I'll line something with him up for this Friday."

Toni grinned as the silence dragged on for a few seconds. Clearly, Audrey was bowled over.

With a squeal, Audrey said, "You kiddin'? After turning up your nose at every guy so far, you've found one you think might pass muster? You go, girl!"

Toni laughed. "Well, I haven't contacted him yet. Could be a dud like all the rest of 'em."

"You know what they say. You gotta be in it to win it! I'm so happy for you, Toni. Really. All work and no play make Jane a dull girl."

"Jane's never dull. Only I am."

"Not true!" Audrey said. "You've got a lot going for you. You just lose sight of it because you deny the vulnerable side of yourself while still being too trusting. That's why you've gotten hurt in the past."

Toni twisted the curly cord of the receiver in her left hand. She suddenly felt very tired. "I suppose you might be right," she said. "Look. I'm bushed. I'm getting off now. Let's just give Lorna some space and see how things work out. Sound like a plan?"

"Sounds like a plan," Audrey said.

The Friday night crowd was in full swing in the restaurant, making it necessary for Toni to raise her voice as she leaned forward over the table to talk to Lorna. After her initial turndown, Lorna relented and agreed to go out with Toni for a girl's night on the town. She said Charles would just have to wing it on his own for the evening. The conversation paused, and they both picked at their appetizers.

Toni didn't mind the brief pause. She allowed herself to relax further as she looked casually around the room. The restaurant was designed with a mixture of black leather banquette seating, brass rails, antique mirrors, and a black-and-white marble floor. It had always struck Toni as being too elegant for a local eatery. The live music of a jazz trio added a positive background vibe throughout the room. In the reflected light, Toni noticed Lorna's shoulders were slumped, her body stiff, and she looked a little pale. No one moved or spoke. After a moment, Toni said something.

"I'm glad you changed your mind and decided to come out and at least have a drink with me. Audrey is on another date with David. I think things are really heating up between them. She wants us to meet him soon. How do you feel about that?"

"Yeah, I'll meet him," Lorna said. "I'm kinda surprised we haven't met up yet. They've been together for more than three months now."

"I know. I think she's been keeping him from us just in case things don't work out. I guess it's almost like a couple not wanting to announce they're pregnant until they're sure the baby is going to be okay."

Toni nibbled on a hot Buffalo chicken wing. The volcanic sauce made her eyes water.

Lorna nodded. "I think you're right." She paused, took a bite of her fried mozzarella stick, dipped the end in the cup of marinara sauce, and took another bite.

"So, what's going on with you and this dating service? You found anyone yet? I know you've been pretty damned picky."

Toni smiled. "Well, I'm corresponding with this guy. I mentioned him before. His name is Donovan. We've been emailing each other and we've exchanged pictures. He just sent me his cell phone number last night. He's nice looking and seems to have all the qualities I'm looking for. So, I think I'll give him a call to at least hear how he sounds."

"Yes, because the kind of luck you have with men, he might sound like Donald Duck."

"That would be the least of my problems," Toni laughed.

Then they both looked at each other and laughed some more. The sound of their laughter echoed throughout the room easing the tension between them.

Toni cleared her throat. "So, um, what's been going on with you and Charles? Is it serious between you two?"

"What do you mean serious? Like we're getting married?"

"Well, yes. That did cross my mind. I mean when a couple chooses to move in together it usually means they're considering taking the relationship to the next level, and in many cases that means marriage."

"No, Charles and I are not about to get married. I'm surprised you would go there."

"Don't be. It's perfectly normal to connect the dots. Audrey and I were a little surprised when we found out he had moved in with you. I know you told us you ran into him, but we didn't think you two were an item again. At least not until you shared the big news with us about him moving in."

Toni remembered Charles had a reputation as a notorious playboy. Although he majored in marketing and attended some classes with them in college, he didn't go into marketing after he graduated. Instead, he drifted from job to job. Lorna had run into him one day after a client meeting. It seemed Charles worked in the same building. They met for dinner a few times, and the old fire in the relationship was quickly rekindled. Toni didn't know why Charles had moved in with Lorna, but she hoped to find out.

"We went out a few times and realized we still had feelings for each other, and the rest, as they say, is history. We decided to move in together. That's all there is to it. No big deal."

Lorna paused. Toni sensed she was deep in thought, and she had something else to say about Charles.

"I realize things might be moving a little too fast," Lorna said. "But, hey, who has time to mess around with dating? Right? Like you! So far, I haven't seen you jumping into the deep end of the pool."

"I know you haven't, but that's all about to change."

Lorna took a sip of her drink. "So you say."

"I mean it. I'm gonna call Donovan. You'll see."

"Suffice it to say I'm not holding my breath."

Lorna looked down at her empty plate of mozzarella sticks. "You know," she said with a sigh, "I never fell in love with anyone else after Charles and I originally broke up. No man ever lit me up inside like Charles did, but now that he's back in my life I'm scared of getting hurt again."

Toni agreed. It was hard to get back on the proverbial horse after getting thrown off and stomped on. That was one big reason why she'd been taking it slow with Donovan.

"I know how you feel," Toni said. "I feel the same way. It's like we're stupid or something, like a kid who touches a hot stove. The kid gets burned, but touches the stove again anyway. Go figure. I guess we sisters are real gluttons for punishment."

Lorna laughed, shook her head.

"So, what's he's doing with his life now?" Toni asked. She was concerned, especially after Lorna had requested a week off from work. She sensed, like Audrey, something was wrong.

"He's in sales."

"Oh, I see."

Toni sat back and stirred her drink. Then she said, "It's just that everyone has noticed how you've changed lately, Lorna, especially after getting involved with him again.

You're not the happy-go-lucky person we know. We're just trying to figure out if everything is alright."

"I'm okay."

Toni gazed at her. "Are you sure?"

"Yes. Thank you all for your concern."

"You know Audrey and I are here for you."

"Yes, I know." Lorna nodded. "Charles and I are very happy. I know when we were in college he used to fool around with other women, but we were younger way back then. He grew up, and he's changed."

She sounded convincing, but Toni sensed a little hesitation. Just then, Lorna's cell phone rang. She pulled it out of her purse and checked the ID, but didn't answer.

"It's Charles. I gotta go. I told him I'd meet him at the club later." Lorna stood, put on her jacket, and grabbed her bag. "Thanks for the drink."

Toni watched as Lorna hurried toward the exit. The jazz group had taken a break and Toni listened to the quick reverberation of Lorna's high heels on the marble floor. She saw her talking on her cell phone, stop, and take a tissue from her purse. She dabbed at her eyes, and then she disappeared through the front door. Was Lorna crying?

4

Audrey stretched her naked body, cat-like, on the Egyptian cotton sheets, and then gazed over at her reflection in the standing oval mirror in her bedroom. Her petite figure, beautiful head of locks, full lips, and perky breasts made her look younger than her thirty-six-years. A minute later, realization slid over her like a black oily film as a memory came flashing back.

She'd had a few great dates with David, and then their relationship changed, moving beyond mere friendship. One evening at a restaurant, she'd been drinking rather heavily. Soon they were talking about kinky sex and sex toys. Without warning, David brought his left hand around and began stroking Audrey down her leg. As the heat passed between then, it was hard for Audrey to keep her hands off him. They kissed as his hand continued exploring her body. Then one thing led to another, and they ended up in Audrey's apartment.

As soon as they got in the door, she began unbuttoning his shirt. In moments, a trail of shed clothing led to her bedroom. Stripped down to her underwear, David asked her to keep her high heels on. He leaned her back on the bed as she watched him unfasten her bra before easing it off. Then they started kissing, his mouth soft and sweet on top of hers. David slowly massaged her thighs until she gasped for breath.

Now, alone in her bedroom, she relived the romantic encounter yet again. The cold chill of regret chased the warmth away. She'd given herself away too quickly. She'd known it at the time, and she hadn't cared. The passion was so intense she wanted nothing more than to surrender to his touch. She chided herself as being weak, too afraid of being alone to stand on her own two feet without needing a man to make her whole. She felt the love she had given away to all those men in her life was wasted. Usually, when she slept with a man so soon after they met, he never stuck around. Already, it occurred to her that David only wanted to take her out to dinner, and then back to her apartment for sex.

She had been physically attracted to David from their first date. He was not only drop-dead gorgeous, but he had a good job and all the personality qualities she desired in a man—intelligence, charm, and wit. Five years younger than her at the age of thirty-one, he'd started his career as an attorney working with one of Atlanta's most experienced family law firms. He was made a junior partner very quickly, and yet he was relatively humble when he mentioned such a stupendous accomplishment for an attorney who was still so young.

But, and there always seemed to be a but, after that drunken scene at the restaurant and in bed afterward it began to dawn on Audrey that David might not be such a great catch. He might be a distraction from her dedication to the business, to herself. She pulled the covers close up under her chin after turning over on her back. David certainly had put a spell on her. It was as if he'd spiked her drinks to take advantage of her, but she knew he hadn't done that. He hadn't needed to. She'd played right into the situation with all the willingness of a silly kid.

Audrey glanced at the clock radio on her nightstand.

"Crap," she said. "Okay, girl! Get your skinny butt out of bed right this minute.

Yawning, Audrey pushed the blanket off, swung herself off the edge of the bed. When her feet hit the hardwood floors in her master suite, she felt the cold of the early morning. The central heat switched on, forcing hot air out of the vents. The sun wasn't up yet. Audrey sighed as she stalked into the bathroom. She was convinced it was going to be another very long day at the office.

Audrey showered and dressed. She ate a bagel with cream cheese and drank a cup of instant coffee black with no cream or sugar, and she began to feel slightly better. Why should she persecute herself for having a good time in bed? She and David were adults. She knew they both wanted what happened. She put the mug and plate in the dishwasher, grabbed her coat, and took the elevator down to the parking garage. She got into her flashy red BMW and started up the engine.

As she pulled out of her high-rise condo building, she actually smiled. Mood swings were not something that were unusual for her. She'd become a master at monitoring her emotions, even her thoughts. She understood people had much more power to control how they felt about the world and how they responded to it than they thought they did. If you realized you were falling into negative self-talk, you could make a conscious decision to shoo it away and replace it with positive self-talk. Maybe, just maybe, she'd let herself go negative for no good reason at all. She thought that was a distinct possibility.

As she merged onto the loop, or the Perimeter, as the locals referred to the freeway that encircled Atlanta, she actually started humming the melody to "Let's Get Married," a hit R&B tune just out from the band Jagged Edge. Suddenly, she couldn't wait to tell the girls about her weekend with David. She'd tell them such a story they'd turn green with envy. Of course, she'd leave out the part where she and David did the deed. Some things were nobody's business.

Toni poked at her house salad with her fork, her thoughts in a whirl. She speared a cherry tomato and ate it. Audrey sat across from her in a corner booth at Pittypat's Porch. Toni noted her partner and best friend looked whipped, and for good reason. Alicia, the office manager had called out because she had to take her mom, who was recovering from a heart attack, to see her cardiologist. Alicia was hardly ever absent, and everyone felt it when she was out for whatever reason. As usual, it was the admins that kept the C-level suite personnel on the straight and narrow. Without support staff, executives like her and Audrey would never get anything done, and Toni was keenly aware of that. That's why she offered generous salaries, three weeks of paid vacation, health benefits, and a matching 401(k) plan. *Atlanta Magazine* designated Toni Summers and Associates as one of the best places to work in the city in 1999, and Toni was really proud of that.

"What a day," Toni said as she forked a cucumber. "I feel like I've been run over by a truck."

"Me too," Audrey said. "What a pain in the butt it is when we have to run shorthanded while we're on a tight deadline."

"Tell me about it," Toni said. She finished her salad and pushed the plate to the edge of the table. "Alicia's worth her weight in gold, and whenever she's out we get a reminder."

Toni moved on to her entre, poached salmon with assorted gourmet vegetables. She took a bite, found the flavors exactly to her liking.

"What do you suppose is up with Lorna?" Audrey asked. "She's been calling in sick a lot lately. I'm really beginning to worry about her."

"We sure could've used her help today. I can tell you that!" Toni said. She paused to eat more of her dinner. Looking over at Audrey, Toni said, "I think there's trouble in River City with Charles. If you ask me, I'd say that's probably it. Did you see that bruise on her right arm the other day when she took off her suit jacket?"

Audrey nodded. "Yeah, and I asked her about it and she said she ran into a door in the dark. You notice how fast she put the jacket back on! It's like she was embarrassed, or like she was trying to hide it from us."

Toni knew what Audrey was thinking. She thought the same as well. "I think Charles might be beating on her," Toni said.

"Maybe we both need to have a long talk with her."

"I agree with you, but you know Lorna, she'll try to dodge the issue," Toni said. "This absenteeism is beginning to affect her relationships with her clients. And her bad attitude is starting to really piss me off."

"Okay, let's set up a meeting with her for one day next week. I'd sure hate to think you're right, Toni, but frankly nothing surprises me these days." Audrey removed her compact from her handbag and freshened up her makeup. "So, tell me, what's been happening with you and Donovan? Have you two agreed to meet yet?"

"We've decided to meet this Friday after work. I feel so nervous. I was wondering whether you and David would be willing to double date? Help break the ice."

"Sorry, sweetie, we won't be able to make it. David has tickets to a jazz concert." She clapped her hands together. "But I have an idea! After you and Donovan have met a few times, then maybe David and I can meet you guys for a special occasion. That way I can check him out and see if he seems sincere or not."

"Okay, I only hope things go well," Toni said. Sometimes I think the hassle of it all is why I just don't bother."

"I know what you mean, but the rewards can make the hassle worth it. Like David and I had a really great weekend. Really great!"

Toni cocked her head, raised an eyebrow. Yeah? How great?" she asked, nursing a sneaking suspicion things had suddenly gone to the next level with Audrey and her new beau. She knew Audrey was a fairly private person, but if Audrey wanted to share more about her relationship with David, she would. If she didn't, that was fine too. Toni had long ago learned that to maintain a solid partnership with Audrey and Lorna she had to give them each enough space to feel as autonomous as possible. As the majority stakeholder in the company, she could have her way on any decision, but she made sure that the leadership style she employed was democratic in nature, as opposed to taking on the more traditional autocratic command-and-control leadership style.

"Like outta this world great!"

"You think he's a keeper?"

Audrey took a sip of her martini, set the glass down, and looked Toni directly in the eye. "I'm really not sure. Part of me wants to lose myself in him, and let him run the show. Part of me wants to feel protected, loved, nurtured, pampered … you know what I mean? And then another part of me feels like a sucker for even thinking like that. I'm not beholden to any man, and I don't like feeling like I'm giving myself up to him without knowing how he really feels about me. Some guys are terrific actors. I've been played like a violin one too many times, if you ask me. I'm totally not into any repeat performances."

Toni understood all too well. "All these emotions are perfectly natural," she said. "Don't fight them. I'm trying not to fight mine. Sometimes you just got to go with the flow, girl."

"And how's that working out for you?"

Toni laughed. "Not well. I think one of the big problems we both have is we don't want to stand in any man's shadow. And for many men that's a big *problemo*. Strong women intimidate some guys. You think David's like that?"

Audrey shook her head and said, "No, he's pretty sure of himself. Sometimes to a fault. A smartass sassy lawyer an all. I tell you what, though. I think he knows he puts a spell on me when I'm with him. It's actually a little scary. I don't feel like I'm in total control, and I don't like it one bit. But, hey, I guess it goes with the territory if you let someone into your life."

"Uh-huh," Toni said, nodding. "That's usually how it goes."

The pretty young server, a brunette with emerald-green eyes, appeared at the table with a tray upon which were two glasses of red wine.

"Sorry, but we didn't order any wine," Toni said. "There must be some kind of mistake."

The server set the glasses of wine in front of Toni and Audrey. "I know you didn't order this, but that guy over there did." She glanced off to the right in an exaggerated gesture. Toni followed the server's glance and saw Scotty Walker grinning at her from his seat at the bar. He was casually dressed in a light-blue Oxford shirt, denim jeans, and a navy blue blazer. Toni had to admit he looked good enough to eat. Scotty came up to the table. Toni smiled at him and said hello.

"Hey, Scotty," Audrey said. "How's it going?"

"Mind if I join you ladies? I could see you were both chatty Kathy an all, but I figured it couldn't hurt to ask if I might sit for a quick visit," Scotty said. "You know. Just shoot the breeze for a bit before we all head on home to hit the sack before we do it all over again. … like in *Groundhog Day*."

"Um, well, it's, uh … how do you know we're not waiting for our dates?" Toni asked, intentionally putting him on. "How do you know Prince Charming isn't on his way right now on a big white stallion? Right this very minute to swoop me off my precious little feet."

"Well, I already thought of that. About your Prince Charming. That's why I waited before I sent over the drinks. Don't wanna be no third wheel. So, I played it cool! I been checking you guys out for the better part of an hour." He looked at his watch. "If you're waitin' on your dates, either they're mighty late or I would say you two have been stood up big time."

Toni looked over at Audrey and laughed. "Can't get anything by you, can we."

Audrey laughed, patted the seat next to her. "Come on, big boy. Plant your sexy butt right here. Take a load off, as they say."

"Don't mind if I do," Scotty said, easing himself into the booth next to Toni.

Toni saw that Audrey noticed how Scotty chose to sit next to her, and not Audrey. Toni caught a slight whiff of Scotty's cologne, and she liked the fragrance. She always had. It was the same cologne he almost always preferred. She felt a slight heat rise within her … the fire of a powerful passion that had not been stoked in a long while. She fakes punched Scotty's right arm and said, "So, how was your day, Mr. Head of Security?"

Toni had left work on Friday evening at around five, went home, freshened up, and changed into a nice beige pantsuit. She was to meet Donovan at seven at an elegant Italian restaurant on Piedmont Street. After she finished getting ready, she drove the short distance to the restaurant, parked in a nearby parking garage, and arrived at the front entrance of the restaurant just before the magic hour. Fighting back her nerves, she went inside and gave the maître d' her name. He seated her at a table tucked away in the corner. The table faced the door, giving her an excellent position to scope Donovan out before he saw her first.

About fifteen minutes later, a tall, clean-shaven man entered the restaurant. She immediately recognized him from his picture, and she was pleasantly surprised to see his photo actually didn't do him justice. He was much more handsome in real life. His online profile said he was six-two and weighed 210 pounds. She was pretty sure that was about right. But the profile picture didn't do justice to his athletic build. He looked like he could be a male model, or an Olympic swimmer. Tall, well-groomed, and sure of himself, he followed the maître d' to her table. His sparkling eyes met hers. His full lips parted into a smile as she stood up to greet him, revealing his almost perfect white teeth.

"You must be Toni?" Donovan asked.

Biting back her nervousness, Toni reached out and shook his hand. "One in the same," she said. "Toni. Toni Summers. Pleased to meet you."

"The pleasure is all mine, I must say," he said, actually giving her a slight bow. "Donovan Tate at your service."

Toni half expected him to gently clasp her right hand in his, raise her hand to his lips, and kiss it, as if she were the queen of England and he was one of her knights in shining armor.

"I'm sorry for being a bit late. Couldn't be helped. Something came up at the office. I'm sure you understand," Donovan said.

"No problem. I wasn't waiting all that long."

"For you!" Donovan said, and handed her a single red rose with a plastic tube filled with water sealed at the base of the long green stem. Some decorative greens were tied up with the rose to make a sort of floral solo arrangement in rose.

"You shouldn't have!" Toni said, warming to him instantly. "It's beautiful." She smelled the flower.

The maître d' grinned. "I'll leave you two alone. Tiffany will be your server tonight. She'll be right over to take your drink order."

"Thanks," Donovan said. He smoothed his suit jacket and sat down across the table from Toni. Toni felt a little weak in the knees. Part of it was nerves. Part of it was her awkwardness around men. She'd never been totally comfortable in the presence of men. Somehow, she felt like she had to submit to the greater male authority, and it made her angry because she hated herself for feeling that way. If a guy was able to break down the brick wall she'd built long ago to protect her from the world and all its cruelties, he had to navigate the complex mix of emotions that constantly swirled around inside her like a giant whirlpool.

Toni primly folded her hands in front of her. She coolly appraised the man seated across from her at the table. She wondered if she'd been a fool to go online to try to find a man, to finally obtain the companionship she'd craved all her life. The death of her parents at such an early age, and then the death of her aunt a few years later had saddled her with a deep-seated fear of being abandoned, of being rejected. She didn't want to be left behind in the bounty of what life could yield. In fact, her drive to succeed in business derived from her insecurities and from her hidden anger at the world at large for causing her so much pain when she was just an innocent kid. In many ways, she'd been over compensating ever since.

"Your profile photo doesn't do you justice," Donovan said.

"Neither does yours," Toni said.

An awkward pause followed, and Toni began to sweat. Maybe she could run away. Maybe she could hurry to the restroom and slip out the back. Obviously, she knew she wasn't about to do that, but the thought definitely flashed through her mind in a moment of initial panic.

"I always hate these first moments," Donovan said. "You know like when you're not sure what to say? And then you say something really dumb?"

Toni felt relieved. She took a sip of her water, fiddled with the napkin in her lap. "Uh, yeah. I totally get what you're sayin'."

"Been on many of these things? Online blind dates, I mean?" Donovan asked.

"First one."

"This isn't my first," Donovan said, "but I'm not exactly an old pro."

The server interrupted to ask for their drink order. Toni was impressed when Donovan handed her the wine list and asked her to make a selection.

"Order anything you like," he said.

Toni noticed the prices ranged from inexpensive to way pricy. She settled on a merlot she knew wouldn't break the bank. Donovan said she'd chosen well, and he suggested they order an appetizer of calamari. The server took their order and left.

She wondered how he knew that calamari was one of her favorite dishes, but then she recalled she'd mentioned it in her online profile. She'd been honest in what she revealed in her profile, and afterward she suffered from buyer's remorse, thinking she'd probably shared too much, that she'd been too trusting and honest in terms of the intimate details she shared about her life, her hopes, her dreams. But, she thought, if she wasn't honest and forthright, then she couldn't expect the man to be either. She felt vulnerable, though, and she didn't like it. She didn't like it one bit.

"Is something wrong?" Donovan asked. "You look like I just farted or something."

That got Toni's attention. "What?"

Donovan laughed. "Oh, nothing."

"What did you just say?" Toni asked, laughing along with him.

"Never mind."

"No, tell me."

"It's just that it seemed like you were a million miles away there for a moment. I was just wondering why."

Toni was about to answer when the server returned with their wine. After she uncorked the bottle and let Donovan sample the wine, she filled their glasses and hurried off. Toni was pleased her initial nervousness dissipated quickly as they exchanged routine small talk, him telling her about his career in software development and her telling him about her career in consumer marketing communications. She could tell he wasn't just playing along as she spoke. He asked intelligent questions about her business model and the types of clients the company specialized in serving.

"I lean toward African-American entrepreneurs," she said, and then took a bit of her appetizer. "We are a typically under-represented community, and I believe we all should stand together in a united way to push forward the black agenda in corporate America. Right now, even in the year 2000, we still got so much work to do I can't freakin' believe it. You see what I'm sayin'? It's like we barely took any steps forward since the civil rights movement back when I was just a wide-eyed little kid."

"I see what you mean. I mean, well, it's like that in tech as well, only probably not so pronounced," Donovan said. "I'm practically the only black dude in the entire IT department, and it makes me feel like I'm letting every other black coder down if I fall short."

"Weird how that is, isn't it?"

Toni identified with Donovan. Like her, he was a high-level professional in his chosen field, and yet she realized he was fighting many of the same stigmas, stereotypes, and stressors she contended with every day as a woman of color in a male-dominated field. She fought against feelings of inadequacy, and she reminded herself almost daily of how far and how fast she'd risen to the top of the African-American business community in Atlanta.

"So, tell me," Donovan said. "What made you want to start a public relations firm?"

"I've always been good at sales. Selling myself, actually. I had to sell myself to all the decision-makers as I was growing up. I had to cultivate the right image, or I wouldn't get placed in a foster home, and I wouldn't get lined up for the scholarships I knew I'd need if I wanted to get ahead."

Donovan reached across the table, took her hands in his. "I'm so sorry. When you told me about your childhood, it just about broke my heart."

Toni felt a surge of warmth flow through her. The man's touch set off a pleasing physical and emotional reaction that was strong enough to make her feel momentarily uncomfortable. She withdrew her hands from his just as the server returned with their food. After the server left, she said, "Yeah,

I did have it pretty rough. But so, have plenty of other people. I don't go around bitching and moaning about it. You can't undo the past. You can just learn to live with it, and you can let it inform your decisions going forward. Don't you think?"

"I do think," Donovan said, taking a bite of his steak. "Sometimes we are our own worst enemies. We tell ourselves we can't do something. That we can never succeed. But that's all just plain BS. You only fail if you don't try. You don't fail if you try and then fail, if you know what I mean."

God, how profound is that? she thought.

Toni nodded, said she agreed. "Sometimes believing in yourself is more than half the battle."

"And how!" Donovan said, shooting her a smile.

Toni was surprised at how she seemed to click with Donovan. Her attraction to him on a physical level was unmistakable, but there was an emotional and intellectual substance that set him apart from most other men she'd met in the past.

"Now that's what I like," he leaned in and whispered. "A woman who isn't afraid of taking chances!"

She took comfort in knowing at least he didn't seem intimidated by a woman in charge of her destiny. In her previous relationships, whenever the guys discovered she was a successful businesswoman they usually didn't stick around much longer. She was looking for someone who was comfortable in their career, and with whom she could exchange ideas.

"I'm curious, it must be cool writing software programs," she said.

"I certainly find it stimulating. I have a master's degree in computer programming. About five years ago I got tired of punching a time clock, so I decided to become a consultant. I freelance by advising and designing office management programs for small and large businesses. I've been working long hours on an account for the past three months, including some weekends and evenings, trying to meet my client's deadline. I love the flexible hours and the money is good. With hard work and persistence, I hope to retire by the time I'm fifty."

"Retire at fifty? Now that sounds nice. You must be running a lucrative business."

"Well, you know, a computer is essential for running day-to-day operations."

"We seem to have similar goals and aspirations," she said. "Tell me, who has been the biggest influence in your life?"

He closed his eyes for a moment, and then said, "I would have to say my father. I was an only child and my dad was a master sergeant in the army. He was a strict disciplinarian. Everything in our household had to be done his way. If things weren't perfect, it was unacceptable. My mom was the one I could go to for a little respite when I needed it." He stopped to refill their wine glasses.

"I remember when I was eight years old my father sat me down and told me he expected me to become either a lawyer, a doctor, or to own my own business. He instilled in me strong work ethics, and said education was the only way to go. I guess I had no choice but to make something of myself. It was a little lonely growing up, though. With my family moving around so much, I didn't develop too many friendships. So, by the time I was nineteen, I married my first girlfriend, and, boy, my father wasn't too thrilled about that! When my marriage ended two years later, I was devastated and blamed him for the control he had over me. I never remarried or had any children." He paused, averting his eyes, and said, "I guess this is too much information for a first date, isn't it?"

"No, not at all. I'm glad you feel comfortable enough to share."

"How about you, who was your biggest influence?" he asked.

Toni remembered what Audrey told her about the importance of being open and honest as she spoke.

"Oh, I'd have to say my guardian, Aunt Gloria was my biggest influence, even though she died when I was only five."

Donovan said, "Yeah, so you said in one of your emails. About her dying when you were so young, I mean. Like I said, I'm so sorry."

Toni swallowed hard and fought back the tears that suddenly threatened to come. "Thanks," she said, her voice barely above a whisper. "It's still hard to talk about it sometimes. Anyway, Aunt Gloria raised me the only way she knew how. She was single and pro-women. Even at a young age, I understood I should not allow myself to be judged by my gender, but by the skills I had to offer. In hindsight, I see why she prepared me to become such an independent woman. I spent the next five years going from one foster home to another. I was very lonely and vulnerable, fighting every day to defend myself. I had to grow up fast."

"I can't imagine what it feels like growing up without a mother and a father."

"Oh, please don't feel sorry for me." She raised her glass, took a sip of wine, and continued. Although she'd shared some of the most important aspects of her life story with Donovan already via email, she went into more detail. She was gratified to see how he listened to every word, and that he asked good questions from time to time as she spoke. She repeated how she'd gone into business with Audrey and Lorna, and the venture capital needed to start the company came mostly from her.

Donovan raised his eyebrows. "Sounds to me like the three of you were pretty tight to go into a partnership together."

"Yes, they're pretty much the sisters I never had. So, here I am today. But the scars never really go away," she said.

"Yeah, I know exactly what you mean." He paused, finished up his baked potato. "Being a success … going into business with your two best friends … I think that's a good way to honor your parents. They would be proud of how you turned out."

"I hope so."

"Oh, I know so. Trust me. They'd be tickled pink to know how far you've come."

The conversation lightened up after that, which was fine with Toni. Things had gotten a bit too heavy for her liking, and yet the deep emotional and physical appeal of the man made her want to share whatever was on her mind. As it turned out, they shared more in common than the same entrepreneurial spirit. They also enjoyed going to concerts, museums, and poetry readings. The dinner ended with a fancy dessert of tiramisu and coffee. When they were finished, he paid the bill, and then helped Toni on with her jacket.

"Let me walk you to your car," Donovan said.

They were silent as they entered the parking lot, and Toni bit her lip. *Will he kiss me goodnight?*

He held the car door open for her as she got in. There was no kiss. He smiled, told her to get home safe, and he said he'd call. Toni believed he would. The evening had gone much better than she could have ever hoped for. She fired up the engine and drove out of the parking lot, seeing Donovan wave in the rearview mirror. A short time later, she pulled into her parking garage and headed to her condo. She could not put her finger on it, but something about Donavan seemed too good to be true. Was it possible she didn't feel like she deserved to be happy? Didn't deserve a truly good man?

Nonsense, she thought as she rode the elevator up to her floor, got out, and unlocked her front door. She tossed her jacket on the sofa and picked up the phone, hoping to share the results of her date with Audrey. The call went straight to voicemail.

5

Lorna strolled into the living room and sat down next to Charles on the sofa. The TV was tuned to the local news. She noted Charles merely gave her a quick sideways glance, yet another sign of his increasing indifference towards her. He didn't even say hi. Somewhat annoyed at being given the cold shoulder for no good reason, she asked him what he wanted for dinner.

"Oh, I dunno," he said, still staring straight ahead at the TV screen. "Whatever."

"That's not helpful, you know. Seriously, what'd like to eat? You have to tell me. I'm no mind reader. I just thought you'd like—"

"Yeah, that's your problem," he snapped. "Why can't you ever make up your mind? How did you ever manage to exist before I came along, anyway? Do me a favor, stop thinking, and start doing."

"I don't even know what to make of what you just said, except it's BS. You've been a real jerk lately. You know that? A real first-class jerk!" Lorna got up from the couch and stormed into the kitchen. Standing at the sink, she took several deep breaths to calm herself down.

Charles had changed considerably since moving in with Lorna. Whenever he came home, all he wanted to do was watch TV. She could scarcely believe what was happening, but it was getting harder to ignore his unpredictable behavior. In the beginning, she had really enjoyed spending time with him, but noticed their passion had decreased lately, and she wasn't sure why. As he became more and more distant, he often pushed her emotionally and physically away whenever she wanted to be close with him. Lorna hoped once he started working again they'd both be happy together.

Charles had been fired from his last job for something that was supposedly not his fault. Apparently, he'd convinced the president of the company to make some procedural changes that would save money for the corporation. Charles's supervisor felt like Charles had upstaged him, made him look bad, and, in response, his supervisor trumped up bogus charges accusing him of being consistently late for work. He got sacked a few weeks later.

Without any steady income, Charles quickly got behind in paying his bills on time, and he'd already maxed out his credit cards. Lorna knew Charles never had been good with money. Once she complained to him about his failure to meet his obligations, and he got really angry with her. It wasn't the first time she'd seen him lose his temper, and it wouldn't be the last. It didn't surprise her when he'd asked if he could move in with her just until he got back on his feet, and she'd agreed to help him out. Secretly, she hoped living together would move the relationship closer to one with more permanence and commitment. At the time, she thought marriage might be a possibility, but she wanted to take it one step at a time. She was in no hurry, and now she wondered if the relationship would even last.

Lorna went to the cabinet above the counter, opened it, and took out a bottle of bourbon. She poured herself a few fingers neat, and felt the warmth of the alcohol as she took her first sip. Resigned to the tension in the condo, she decided to take a walk to clear her head. She headed back into the living room … and stopped dead. Not believing her own eyes, she watched as Charles snorted a long line of coke right off the coffee table.

"You don't have money for rent, but you have money for blow?" Lorna asked, her hands on her hips, her anger rising by the second. "I don't want drugs in my house, Charles. I mean it. This behavior is unacceptable!"

"The hell it is," he said, glaring at her.

Lorna was surprised at the intensity of his expression. It scared her a little. Charles quickly stood up and came at her. She backed up.

"Charles! What the hell are you doing?"

Before she could react any further, he grabbed her by the shoulders and throw her hard down on the couch.

"You're not the boss of me!" he screamed, backing away slightly and raising his right fist. "Nobody's the boss of me!"

"You're gonna regret what you just did," she said, seething with rage.

"Yeah, sure."

Lorna got up, pushed past him, and walked deliberately into the master suite. She opened the door to the walk-in closet and yanked Charles's suitcase off the bottom shelf, and then she went into the bedroom and threw the suitcase on the bed. She opened the dresser and started emptying the drawers of everything that belonged to Charles.

"Just what the hell do you think you're doing?" he asked, coming up behind her.

Lorna whirled around. "You stay back! Stay away. I want you outta here right now. Right this minute! I never should've trusted you to change. You're the same as you always were."

She continued throwing his stuff in the suitcase. Charles slapped her hard across her right cheek … hard enough to see stars as she lost her balance and fell. Searing pain shot through her left knee and elbow.

"You can't throw me out!" he shouted. "I have nowhere else to go!"

Charles took hold of her collar, lifted her back to her feet, and threw her on the bed. She landed hard enough to feel winded. She struggled for breath. Her heartrate soared as she jumped up and kicked Charles in the balls. She noted with pleasure how his eyes suddenly got wide in a millisecond, and a momentary look of shock and disbelief showed clearly on his face. He groaned, clutched his crotch, and doubled over in pain. Lorna ran to the phone and called the cops.

Wrapped in a big white towel after taking a long hot shower, Lorna studied herself in the mirror over the sink. The harsh overhead light above the sink accentuated the bruises on her face, particularly around her right eye. She ran a shaky hand over her clammy forehead. She spotted a few fresh bruises on both of her upper arms. She started blow drying her hair, and she felt ashamed. After the police came to her condo, Lorna had refused to file an official report of domestic violence against Charles. Although she knew it was foolish, she blamed herself for provoking him.

Later, during their zealous lovemaking-makeup session, only the soft, sweet taste of his lips and the warm safety of his arms around her mattered.

She closed her eyes, recalling her turmoil. If someone had told her back then she would end up dating Charles again, she would never have believed them. All her dreams and expectations she once had of marrying him during her college years had vanished. As the tears threatened to flood her eyes again, she blinked them back.

How long is this going to go on?

Lorna knew she had a serious problem, and she wasn't sure how to deal with it. In a way, she felt frozen, powerless, and dependent on Charles all at the same time. The mix of emotions was intense, and her moods swung wildly from moment to moment. And she had trouble controlling her feelings.

Glancing at her watch, she quickly brushed her teeth, splashed some cold water on her face, brushed her hair back, and with a little bit of ingenuity applied her makeup to conceal the bruises on her face. The makeup combined with sunglasses would do the trick, or so she hoped. She went into the closet and reached for a pink pullover sweater and black pants. Then she put on her black flat shoes, grabbed her purse and car keys, and quickly left for work before Charles woke up.

The drive to the office went quickly. She hustled into the building, rode the elevator to the fifteenth floor, and hurried into the conference room with her coffee.

"Holy crap! What the hell happened to you?" Audrey asked.

"Don't try telling us you ran into a door again," Toni said. "We know what's going on."

Lorna sat down and sighed. She suddenly felt exhausted. "It was nothing. Charles and I had a little disagreement. I guess I got on his nerves."

"It was nothing! That's bullshit!" Audrey jumped to her feet. "That's a black eye, and you don't get a black eye by getting on someone's nerves."

"Tell us the truth, Lorna," Toni interjected. "Is he abusing you? First, we noticed the bruise on your arm, and now this. It seems to me this has been going on for some time. Did you call the police?"

"Yes. I called the police, but like I said it was a minor misunderstanding.

Charles is going through a rough time right now, and I don't want to add more to his stress by pressing charges."

"Are you insane? You are the victim here and he deserves to spend some time in jail. Why are you defending him? Hell, he wasn't feeling sorry for you when he was smacking you around. He could've killed you," Audrey said.

"Well, he didn't. So, can we get on with the meeting? I have to leave early today. I have a doctor's appointment."

Audrey shrugged, and sat back down.

Toni said nothing. She began the meeting by passing Lorna a binder.

"Before we get started, Lorna, we wanted to discuss a few things with you," Toni said. "You've been a worthy and dependable partner, and your clients praise you. But in the past few months you really haven't been on top of your work, and because of that your ethics have become very sloppy. You've been coming in late and leaving early. You've missed some important deadlines. We can't continue giving your clients excuses as to why you're not available when they call."

Lorna pushed her sunglasses up to the top of her head, touching her fingers together nervously, she attempted to crack a smile. "So, what are you saying? Are you attempting to buy me out of the company?"

"No, that's not what we're saying," Toni said.

"I've been hearing rumors about you two wanting me out."

"I know you may have been hearing rumors about a potential buyout, but we would like to come to some kind of resolution that will suit us all. I mean, we have to consider what is best for the company. We've come too far to allow it to fail."

Audrey tapped the table with the tip of her pen. She put the pen down and leaned back in her chair. "Toni is right. We don't want to buy you out. Personally, I'd prefer to see you get rid of Charles. He's just bringing you down. Can't you see that?"

Lorna grew increasingly agitated about Audrey getting into her business. Who was she to talk about her boyfriend like that? Besides, Lorna knew once Charles got his life back on course everything would be fine between them, or at least that was what she tried to convince herself of. At times like these, though, it was pretty tough to think anything would significantly change for the better.

"I'm very sorry if I haven't been holding up my end of the bargain, and I'm most appreciative of Alicia taking some of my workload. I'll make it up to her." Lorna turned to Audrey and said, "No disrespect, but you of all people shouldn't be acting like judge and jury. I don't tell you who you should or should not date, or sleep with, and I don't expect you to tell me."

"I wasn't trying to judge you. We don't want to see you get hurt, that's all," Audrey replied.

"Well, I'm *not* going to kick Charles to the curb, especially when he's down."

Toni had been watching the banter between her friends for a while, and felt she needed to intercede before it got out of hand. "Okay, Lorna, so what do you suggest we do with your accounts? I mean short of reducing your workload even further what can we do?"

Lorna rubbed her palms together rapidly and exclaimed. "I'll stay in touch with the two clients I've already been working with! As a matter-of-fact, I'm having lunch with Danielle Simmons from Matrix Media tomorrow."

"Okay. Good. What's going on with the other account, Sun Fusion, Inc?"

"That account is going great, too. We've been communicating over the phone regularly. They seem quite pleased with our agency."

"Great," Toni said. "Now, about your two new accounts. Is there any way we can get Alicia more involved with them?"

Lorna didn't like where the meeting was going, but deep down she realized she needed to scale back until things settled down at home. She opened a file, and then looked over at Toni.

"Alicia can work with the two new accounts. I'll fill her in on the details and introduce her as my contact. But it's important to know there may be times when I need to work from home, and I'm going to need your support on this."

Toni turned to Audrey. "What do you think about this arrangement, Red? My main concern is the clients come first."

Audrey crossed her arms over her chest. Lorna noticed she looked briefly annoyed, and then her face relaxed a bit. "I agree," she said sternly. "The clients should always come first."

"Good. It makes life easier when we're all on the same page," Toni said.

Before Lorna could respond, her cellphone rang. She swung around in her chair and answered it. "Hello? Yes, I'll be there in twenty-minutes."

Lorna stood up, and put on her sunglasses. "Something's come up. I have to leave. I'll see you guys tomorrow."

And she quietly walked out the door.

Audrey slid to the edge of her chair and leaned forward. "Oh, my God! Please tell me that didn't just happen."

"Well, apparently it did," Toni said.

"Why didn't you take a stronger stand with her? I would've thought you'd let her know just how things are getting bad with her. Bad enough to maybe induce us to buy her out, if it comes to it."

"I didn't want to come on too strong. At least not yet anyway. Lorna is going through a lot right now," Toni said. "I think she's being abused by Charles. That much seems pretty obvious."

Audrey nodded in agreement. "Yeah, I believe so, too. Lorna has a right to her own decisions and choices, whether they're right or wrong. As her friends, we ought to be there to support her through each bump in the road, but we can't keep pacifying her if she chooses to stay with that jerk."

"Just remember, Audrey, this could've happened to you, me, or Alicia. I think we need to handle this situation delicately for now." Toni let out a frustrated sigh. "I only hope it doesn't get too out of hand. I only hope we can get our friend the help she desperately needs."

"So, where do we go from here?" Audrey asked.

"I think I should call our attorney and set up a meeting to discuss this matter with him before the shit possibly hits the fan!" Toni said.

6

Audrey arrived home that evening exhausted. She kicked off her shoes and threw herself down on the couch.

A bath would feel good tonight. If only I had the strength to move.

Finally, forcing herself to get up, she entered the bathroom, ran the water, and dropped in a pellet. She breathed deeply and gave a contented sigh as the room began to steam with the scent of lavender. Slipping out of her clothing, she eased herself into the hot, silky water, savoring the tickle of the steady bubbles on her toes. Resting her head on a mini-pillow, she closed her eyes to unwind and reflected on what transpired earlier in the morning meeting.

She still could not believe Lorna could be so determined to stay with her boyfriend, Charles, after he treated her so badly. This made her think about her new relationship with David. Although they had known each other for three months, she realized she had no idea of his personal likes and dislikes. What if he abused women like Charles? Or worse ... what if he was a serial killer? As soon as she thought that she smiled and shook her head at the absurdity of her line of thinking. Of course, David was trustworthy. While some alarm bells of a vague sort sounded in the back of her mind now and then, overall, she was fine with him. Falling in love, as a matter of fact.

David had told her he was born in Baton Rouge, Louisiana. The youngest of four, he was raised by a single mother. He said, he never knew his biological father. Once he was nine-years-old, his mother told him the story of how he was the creation of an affair. When her husband found out about her infidelity, the marriage was over, and he left her to raise the children alone.

After graduating from high school, David moved to Atlanta to go to Georgia State University, where he majored in law and public administration. Upon passing the bar exam, he started his career as a litigation attorney, and he later went into family law. Lost deep in thought, the ring tone of her cellphone startled her. She saw from the number it was David. She clicked on and they exchanged greetings.

"Looks like I'm going to be stuck at the office for a while. I don't think I can take you out to dinner after all."

For a second, her mind wandered. *Oops, how could I forget?* She was so tired she had completely forgotten about their date. Then she had an idea.

"Why don't you come by after you're done. I'll throw a little something together," she suggested, trying to remember what she had in the fridge.

"But it won't be until around nine o'clock," he said.

"That's fine. It'll be a quick meal."

"Okay, see you then!"

Two hours later, Audrey had prepared a version of pasta primavera with a box of bowtie pasta and frozen vegetables. Dressed in a long black skirt and a white halter top, she sipped a glass of wine while relaxing on the couch. She clicked off the television when her intercom buzzed downstairs. When David appeared at her front door, she smelled his Brut cologne first. The fragrance was a fusion of minty leaf and the subtle zest of lavender. Dressed in a white Oxford shirt and a pair of jeans, he was holding a bottle of red wine. She wondered if he did indeed just come from work.

"Hi, handsome," Audrey said. "Come on in!" She made a sweeping gesture with her right arm and nodded toward the living room. "Is this how you normally dress for work?"

He smiled, kissed her cheek, and handed her the bottle of wine. "For you. No, for us! To answer your question, I don't wear jeans at work. That wouldn't be professional. As I'm sure you can imagine, attorneys put in a ton of hours. When things are really busy, it's not unusual for me to log eighty hours."

She said, "Wow! And I thought we worked hard. Hey, come into the kitchen and I can uncork this sucker."

She turned to go into the kitchen, and David followed.

"So, as I was saying, I keep a set of casual clothes in the office just for occasions like this."

"I always knew you were smart!"

She fished a corkscrew out of a drawer and started to open the bottle.

"Allow me," David said, taking control of opening the wine while she got the glasses.

When the wine was poured, she offered a toast. "To us," she said. They clinked glasses.

"Let me just heat up dinner, and we can eat."

A short time later, Audrey sat across from David as they ate in companionable silence. When they were finished, Audrey collected the paper plates she'd put out and tossed them in the garbage can under the kitchen sink. She poured the rest of the wine into their glasses and padded into the living room, where she plopped down on the sofa. She patted the seat next to her, and David sat down. She could feel the warmth of his skin. The cologne tantalized her.

Stay cool, girl!

Audrey suddenly thought about Lorna, her black eye, the fact she seemed to always be distracted about one thing or another, and that Charles was proving to be a bad addition to her friend's life. She sighed, shook her head.

"What?" David asked. "What's up? You seem sad all of a sudden."

Audrey told him about Lorna.

David leaned back on the sofa and folded his arms behind his head. "Do they have kids?"

"No, thank God! They're not even married. Just living together."

"Well, if I were your friend, I would get the hell out of that relationship quick. Abusive relationships can be dangerous. Everyone knows that. It can also be hard for the victim to leave the relationship out of fear and dependency."

"I think that could be the case with Lorna."

"Unfortunately, it's her decision to make. I'm sorry to say her situation is likely to get much worse before it gets better."

Audrey swirled the last of the wine in her glass into a miniature whirlpool, and then she finished the wine off with a backward toss of her head. She set the glass down on the coffee table and looked over at David, who was seated with his legs crossed, his left arm extended outward along the back of the couch.

God, he looks good enough to eat, she thought.

As if he'd read her mind, he leaned in close and began massaging her shoulders. She closed her eyes, feeling her entire body relax at his touch.

"Dinner was delicious!" he said. "I thought this would be a good treat for you."

"Hmmm. It does feel great." She inhaled slowly.

In the next moment, he pulled her close and rested her head against his chest. His breath hot and urgent, he nibbled at her ear lobe while whispering soft words in between his kisses. "You know you drive me wild!" he said, his voice low and husky.

Audrey bit her lower lip nervously, the butterflies in her stomach going crazy. She turned around to face him. Then he captured her mouth with his. As his lips parted, their tongues met in a dance. She returned the kiss with fervor. From that instant on, nothing else mattered.

He gently scooped her into his arms and carried her into the bedroom. Once inside the bedroom, he sat her down on the bed and slowly untied her halter top. He then helped her remove her skirt. It dropped to the floor. Audrey trembled at his gentle touch as he swooped his hands up to cup her breasts.

"Oh, my!" he smiled. "You're so beautiful. So perfect. So damned sexy!"

As she unzipped his jeans, she whispered, "You are so bad. Real bad! I can see you are really happy to see me!"

"Damn right!" he said. "I would think that'd be pretty obvious."

He gently laid her onto the bed and they began to make love. Audrey savored the warmth of his body pressed against hers. Raging in the heat of passion, the momentum of their lovemaking picked up. Her cries of pleasure matched his. She grabbed the bedpost with both hands, arched her back, and shouted, "Yes, yes, yes!"

Seconds later, he yelled out, "Oh, God!"

She felt him envelope her in his embrace which grew less ardent as their passion faded with time. She felt his heart beating hard, the wet warm moisture of his sweat. In silence, they lay side by side. She felt satiated, satisfied, and loved. She rested her head against his chest, felt the rise and fall as he breathed. The bedroom was still filled with the scent of his cologne, but there was also the unmistakable odor of sweat and sex.

"Wow!" he said. "You were something else! As always."

"So were you," she said, and she inexplicably felt a wave of sadness that confused her. She didn't understand why her emotions swung so quickly in the opposite direction of where they were just moments earlier. Perhaps, she thought, it was she didn't trust in the relationship … not fully. She wondered if she ever would be able to give herself so completely to another human being that trust would be unconditional, the love based on love itself and nothing else. Not based on unfulfilled expectations from past failed relationships. Not based on financial or professional ceilings. She listened to David falling asleep, and she turned her head into the pillow, away from David, just as hot tears began to trickle down her cheeks.

7

Toni let the hot jets of water from the shower gently massage her face. She gazed up, her eyes closed, and tried to calm her already tumultuous thoughts in preparation for what she knew would be a very hectic day. As she lathered up, she considered whether it was really prudent to have contacted the company attorney, Mr. Lawrence Bentley, a heavyset guy of fifty with a bright smile and a razor-sharp brain that set him apart from most other corporate lawyers in Atlanta. She'd realized long ago that three years of law school only qualified you to rip people off for outrageous legal fees and little or no service in return. Experience, integrity, ethics, honesty, hard work, fairness, and an eagle eye for the crooks and the crooked were what made an attorney worth his or her salt, and Toni knew it. She'd found out the hard way a damned shyster lurked behind every dark corner and under every mossy rock.

She'd found Larry early on, just a year or two after she'd started Toni Summers and Associates in 1995. One of the many things that drew her to him and his law firm—Bentley, Peters, and Washington—was his emphasis on minority business development. Although Atlanta's African-American population outnumbered the white population by at least 10 percent, basically a steady difference over time from census to census, the deck was stacked against black business owners in terms of laws, regulations, loans, property, and capitalization. Venture capitalists favored white businesses. Toni understood why. People like to hang with their own kind. Thus, Larry's connections with black venture capitalists and politicians proved to be invaluable to her as she built her business from the ground up.

In some ways, Larry was the opposite of what one would expect from a legal beagle. When he laughed, he laughed from the belly. He could be reserved and serious when he wanted to be, but he also saw the bright side of life more times than not. He was a glass-is-half-full kinda guy. When he had spare time, he'd dash off to the mountains with some of his drinking buddies, and piss away the days hunting for deer in deer season, and fishing for bass and brook trout whenever he could carve out a slot in his insanely busy schedule.

Larry also loved the theater. A lot. If he hadn't been married for more than a dog's age, she'd have wondered if he leaned the other way in his sexual orientation. She chastised herself for thinking that, telling herself just because a big guy at over two hundred pounds loved musicals didn't mean he belonged to the LGBT community. She'd fallen right into the typical stereotypical view that comes from being ignorant of the true reality any minority experiences in an often intolerant and biased society. Still, she couldn't help but grin when she pictured Larry dancing around onstage like a big black elephant in a tight pink tutu.

Toni finished rinsing off in the shower, feeling a little more like herself. It was odd how doing something as normal as taking a shower could help calm the nerves and usher in a new day. She'd called Larry to discuss Lorna's future with the firm. As important as this meeting was, Toni was reluctant to move forward with it. Although she felt she and Audrey were being secretive having this meeting, the last thing she wanted to do was to leave any stone unturned. A few days earlier, Lorna had notified them she would be working from home again for the rest of the week. Audrey went ballistic, and Toni wasn't pleased either. She finished drying off, got dressed, and put her makeup on. Then she went into the kitchen to make coffee.

As she drank her coffee and scanned the morning paper, she felt sad about how Lorna seemed to be a slave to Charles, a plaything, a boxing bag. Just hearing her downplay the abuse from Charles was too much to endure. It had never occurred to Toni that Lorna was so desperate to have a man in her life that she'd lower herself in such a way as to become a pawn in another person's twisted psychological chess game. Little by little, Toni thought, her best friend was losing her identity and becoming something not of her own making, but of Charles's.

She'd always imagined Lorna to be a strong woman, but, maybe, her life was just a reflection of what it used to be after all. Maybe Lorna was weak and flawed, and had been from the start. Maybe Lorna had been so successful because she was able to hide herself from the world, and even hide herself from herself. It was a sobering and depressing thought.

Toni sighed. "Oh, hell," she said, "there's nothing you can do about the bastard. Lorna, girl! You best grow a pair! Throw Charles the hell out of your life."

She stood up from the kitchen table, put her coffee mug in the dishwasher, and hurried to get her coat. Although spring was now in the air, it being early March, it was still cold in the predawn hours. Even though her heart felt heavy, she considered herself lucky being raised by two strong women who led by example—her maternal aunt, and her adoptive mother. She would never allow any man to treat her in such a demeaning and abusive way, but Lorna definitely didn't seem ready to stand up for herself, and, as a consequence, she was letting Toni and Audrey down, not to mention the two big clients on Lorna's priority list. Hence the meeting with Larry.

Toni shrugged on her coat, snatched her purse from the table in the foyer, and rushed down to the parking garage. She fired up the Porsche and was soon on the Perimeter heading south, looping around the big city to Larry's office in Roseland. Her thoughts continued racing. She thought her first date with Donovan had gone well. They had a great conversation, and they'd certainly flirted with each other a little. It was nice when he called her later to say he had a good time. She had been thinking about him ever since. Although she welcomed a second date, they couldn't pinpoint a time because of their hectic schedules. He promised to call her in a few days. She figured he would.

The ride to Roseland went fast. She arrived at Larry's office at eight o'clock sharp, and the receptionist showed her in. Larry smiled broadly as he stood up from behind his desk and came around to greet her with a brief hug and a tiny peck on the cheek.

"Toni, how the hell are you!" he said, standing back.

"Can't complain, really," Toni said. "Of course, there's always something going on."

"Ain't that the truth," Larry said. "Tell me about it."

Larry gestured to the large leather sofa in the sitting area. "Have a seat," he said. "Coffee? Tea?"

Toni shook her head. "No, thanks. I'm good."

Toni sat down, looked around. It had been almost a year since she'd been in Larry's office. He usually came to her, but she decided to come see him rather than have him go to her. Not that Lorna would've known. After all, she was working from home for the rest of the week, which, truth be told, was one of the last straws to break the proverbial back of the camel. Alicia, however, would have wanted to know why Larry was meeting with them, and Toni didn't want that either. She'd left Audrey to hold down the fort. She'd let Audrey know the outcome of the meeting when she returned to the office later that morning.

Not much had changed in almost a year. The office décor remained traditional, even stark. The furnishings were dark wood, classic American. Very little art adorned the walls. She noted the giant stuffed brook trout still occupied a prominent place over the wet bar. Pictures of Larry with his wife, Liz and their two beautiful now grown girls, sat alongside the knickknacks and books on an ornate hutch that she'd always figured was an antique.

"So, let's get down to brass tacks, shall we?" Larry said. "Remember, be open about any of your concerns. I know it may feel a little uncomfortable discussing one of your partners, but I'm sure you wouldn't have scheduled this meeting if you didn't think it was important."

He looked down at his legal pad. "Now, as the majority shareholder in the company, you are in the driver's seat. You know that, don't you?"

Toni nodded.

"The language in the partnership contract is pretty straightforward. You have the right to buy out either of your best friends at any time for any reason. So, I'm not really clear on what the problem is. If you want Lorna Stanley out, then she's out. Simple as that."

"Maybe not so simple. I don't wanna get sued."

Toni noticed how serious Larry suddenly looked.

"Why would you think Lorna would sue you? If you pay her the fair market price for her shares in the company, I doubt she'd have a problem with the settlement as long as she doesn't feel like she's being pushed out unfairly."

Toni got up from the couch and walked to the window. She took a few moments to gather her thoughts. She gazed at the manicured lawn visible through the expansive windows behind Larry's desk. Two-story offices clustered around a courtyard with benches and a fountain. The usual obligatory live oak with its arching branches and drapes of Spanish moss provided some shade when the sun beat down, especially in the hot humid Atlanta summers.

"I just have a bad feeling about this is all," Toni said, turning to face Larry. "The reason Lorna isn't holding up her end in the company is she's being abused by her jerk of a boyfriend. If we displace her because she's a victim, that's not gonna look too good in front of a judge or a jury if she raises hell about being pushed out and we end up in court."

Toni sat down.

"Well, the two issues are linked, and, then again, they're not," Larry said. "While it's sad she's being abused and that it's hindering her abilities to carry out her duties for the agency, her predicament should have no bearing on company policies and procedures."

"That's how Audrey and I both feels," Toni said.

"You're both right on target. I don't know about you, but I could use some coffee."

Larry got up, went to his desk, and alerted his secretary that he would like some coffee. "You sure you won't join me?" he asked.

Toni said sure. When the coffee came, they sat in silent contemplation for a few minutes.

"Have you tried to get her help? An intervention or something?" Larry asked.

"We've talked to her, but she's so dependent on him she's in denial that she's in a bad, even a dangerous, place. Frankly, Audrey and I feel terrible about even considering buying her out. But when we come to work some of us know how to detach ourselves from our personal lives. Then others are so sensitive that if things are going crazy in their personal lives it interferes with the business at hand. In the past few months, Audrey and I have had to rearrange our schedules to keep up with our clients because Lorna is falling down on the job. I don't think we should use friendship as an excuse to avoid running a professional business. We don't want our company to come to an end because of one person's poor performance."

"Well, a business partnership is like a marriage and it comes with some emotional baggage," Larry said, "and like newlyweds, partners in the beginning are often blindsided by the bright glow of hopes and dreams. No one likes to think of themselves as the negative one in any enterprise, and how we expect people to behave can sometimes result in tension, resentment, and frustration. That's why legal considerations should always be thought of in advance."

Larry paused for a moment to look over his paperwork. "If you wish to proceed, I don't think the abuse question is going to be relevant. I'll need to meet with your accountant to determine the value of your company, and what each partner's share would be worth. This may seem simple, but you're right, we have to be very thorough as there can be consequences. We don't want Lorna suing you later on down the road."

"Yes, that's true," Toni said. "We would want this to end amicably."

Larry pursed his lips and scribbled on his legal pad. "Okay, tell me, what is the most important goal of the company?"

"What do you mean?" Toni asked.

He continued, "What are your long-term objectives for, say, next year?"

"Certainly, profits are a big part of it," she said, "but in our line of business we are always concerned with client satisfaction."

"How often do you measure customer satisfaction to track the results of your profit margins?"

"We do it every six months. Why?"

Larry stirred his coffee again, even though he'd already done it. He sat upright on the sofa, jutting his chin forward as if recalling a previous set of circumstances.

"I'm just speculating that before you make any final decisions on dissolving your partnership with Lorna, you might conduct some customer satisfaction research. You need to be able to answer these important questions to see if Lorna's performance, or lack thereof, has hurt your agency's bottom line."

The same nagging question had pestered Toni for weeks. She wondered if Lorna's behavior really was hurting the agency and jeopardizing its future.

"Ask yourselves some key questions," Larry said. "How satisfied are your customers? Are they more or less pleased with your company this year than they were last year? How does your customer satisfaction level compare with that of your competitors? And, what impact does it have on your company's profits? I'm assuming you trust Alicia with taking over Lorna's accounts, right?"

"Yes, we trust her. She has a background in marketing and statistics," Toni replied.

"Good. Now here's another consideration. I'm sure the customers view your partnership as the driving force behind this business, but if they discovered you were having problems it could be to your disadvantage."

"Yeah, image is everything in PR."

"I suggest you give Lorna three months to get her act together. But let Lorna know what you're doing. Be honest with her. This way, it will help document your reasons for needing to terminate her partnership position in the agency, and it will leave no room for litigation later on. You keep your business running smoothly, and the customers won't even know there was a problem. What do you think?"

"That sounds like a plan!" Toni said. "I think we have enough customer-centered clients to make this work. We'll give it a try."

"I'll work with your accountant to determine the fair market value of your shares, and to negotiate a buyout package, if this is the way we need to go. I'll get back to you in two weeks."

"Thank you for helping us reach a resolution," Toni said, standing up and shaking his hand. "You've given me a lot to think about."

8

Lorna had just finished interviewing her last client, and she felt relieved when she hung up the phone. She was extremely proud of the results as she was glad that she still had a great working relationship with the company.

I need to update my files in the computer.

Having the ability to work from home on occasion was always a nice perk. She was grateful to Toni and Audrey, who were receptive to her idea and agreed to her timetable. Lorna strongly believed her choice to work at home could help improve the relationship between Charles and herself. Every day since he'd lost his job, she'd noticed he could not eat or sleep. Even though they talked about things, they had agreed whatever he was going through was only temporary. Yet, he seemed determined to keep a suitable distance between them. Lorna had updated his resume, and that morning before he left for another job interview, she reassured him things would work out.

Suddenly, a loud slam of the front door startled her. She swiveled around in her chair and stopped for a moment when she caught sight of Charles's open suit jacket, untucked shirt, and the stains on his tie. He had only been gone for two hours, and yet he seemed to have hit rock bottom in that short span of time. Averting his eyes, he abruptly left the room and walked into the kitchen. Lorna was revolted by the smell of cigarettes and alcohol that hung in the air like a cloud.

"Hey, babe. What happened?" she asked, following him to the kitchen.

Charles did not answer, he opened the cupboard, took out a small glass, and pulled out a flask from his inner jacket pocket. She watched him pour a drink of whiskey and gulp it down.

"What do you think happened? I didn't get the job," he answered coolly.

Then he poured another drink, but before he could put the glass to his mouth, Lorna reached out to stop him.

"Charles, don't," she begged.

The glass he held dropped to the floor, shattering to pieces. Immediately, he grabbed her wrists.

"Charles, you're hurting me!"

"Who gives you the authority to tell me what to do?" he said, his eyes boring into hers. "What do I look like? A child?"

He released her wrists, and she bit her lip to keep from crying with the pain. She instinctively stretched out her arms to him. He roughly pushed her aside and stormed into the living room. Lorna trailed behind him. He sat down on the couch, and she sat down next to him.

"Charles, it's unfortunate you didn't get this job but I just don't see any reason for you to drink yourself into a stupor. There will be more job interviews." She clutched his hand in hers for comfort. "Remember when we first met in college? How we shared our dreams and ideas? Well, babe, I wanted a life with you then, and nothing has changed. I understand the pain you're going through and I want you to know I'm still here for you." Maintaining eye contact, she continued. "But I don't understand why you treat me so badly. I really don't. I have done nothing to deserve this shit, and you know it."

Charles remained motionless with his head bowed. Then with a heavy, shuddering movement he raised his head and looked at her. There was something in his eyes, a faint flush in his cheeks, a softening of his mouth.

"I'm sorry, Lorna. I know I've been a fool. It's because I expect everything to go right, and when it doesn't, I feel like a total failure. I know we did so many things together. This may sound dumb, but, honestly, I've been trying to recreate the way things were between us back then. You deserve to have more in a relationship, and I'm willing to try, except I don't know how ..."

Before he finished his sentence, she put her finger to his mouth. "You hush now, babe. I love you so much, and I don't know what else to do but love you. All your faults and everything. I don't care. I'll take you as you are."

Charles hesitated for a moment before he turned and cupped her face in his hands, and then kissed her. His hot lips sent shivers down her spine; her pulse raced. Slowly, she responded as he continued kissing her more and more passionately. Then they parted and she nestled against him with a deep sigh, laying her head on his shoulder. It had been such a long since he'd touched her so gently, and she longed for him.

"I don't want to upset you anymore," he said.

She gazed into his eyes. "I'm not upset with you."

Pressing his lips to her forehead, with his hand cupping the back of her neck, he slid his hand down the neckline of her blouse, undoing the top buttons. He resumed kissing her and she moved her hand to his head, running her fingers through his hair. Switching, he moved his mouth to murmur in her ear. "I think we have some unfinished business to take care of."

Charles stood and helped her to her feet. The moment the bedroom door closed behind them, he reached out to her, pulling her body close against his. They collapsed into each other's arms and sank down onto the bed in a warm embrace. As Charles took charge, she was suddenly unable to speak. Afterwards, he took her in his arms and stroked her hair. She loved the attentiveness she was receiving from Charles. She really loved him and thought they needed each other. As she knew all too well, everything would be better if she just waited for Charles to get his act together. As she lay with him in bed, a flash of self-doubt stabbed at the warm luster of her mood.

What if he doesn't change? What then?

9

Toni was in a hurry. She rushed down the corridor on her way to her office, her briefcase in her right hand, her purse slung over her left shoulder. She was late for a teleconference with one of Lorna's clients. Just before she got to the door of her office, she saw Scotty get off the elevator with a large fancy bouquet of assorted flowers. He smiled at her as he strode over to her and handed her the prize.

"Here, these are for you," he said. His eyes sparkled as he stared at her. "By the way, you look absolutely stunning in that pantsuit!"

"Wow, Scotty, thank you! What's the occasion?"

Relishing the mixed display of lilies of the valley, pink roses, and yellow daffodils, she inhaled deeply, and then she read the attached card, noting with pleasure the flowers were from Donovan, not Scotty.

"Sorry, I wish it was from me," he said.

Did Scotty sound jealous?

"Who's this guy in the lobby? Rather than have him sign in, I told him I would deliver the flowers and let you know he's here."

"Oh, that was very nice of you. He's my lunch date."

Scotty placed his hands in his pant pockets and shifted from one leg to the other.

"Why? Is there a problem?" she asked.

"Not at all," he replied. "I was just wondering how long I've been asking you out on a date. Let's see, one year, eleven days and," he said, looking at his watch for dramatic effect, " ...ten hours." He chuckled. His beeper went off, and he quickly checked it. "Uh-oh, I have to go. This conversation is to be continued! Who knows, maybe one day I'll get lucky and you'll say yes to me. At least once. Just to put me out of my misery."

"Life is full of surprises," Toni said with a smile. "You never know what's gonna happen next. Hey, I gotta go too. Late for a teleconference."

"Guess we're off to the races then." Scotty paused, looked at her intently. "I'm serious about that date, you know."

"Yeah," Toni said, "I know. Do me a favor, Scotty."

"Anything for you."

"Would you tell Donovan, the guy waiting for me in the lobby, I'm on a conference call and he should come on up and wait for me here?"

Scotty looked like he'd just smelled some really rancid Limburger cheese. He said he would tell him. Then they both went their separate ways.

Toni had a difficult time focusing on the teleconference, but she muddled through. When the meeting ended, she hurried to the reception area. Donovan was handsomely dressed in a classic charcoal gray suit with a white shirt accented with a gray and white striped tie. He removed his sunglasses as Toni walked over to greet him. He came forward and gave Toni a hug, and then whispered in her ear. "You look like a million bucks today."

Toni smiled and said, "Why, thank you. You don't look so bad yourself."

She chose to dress casually in a tailored forest green pantsuit with a white ruffled blouse, and fancy green and black heels. As Donovan placed his hand on her arm and escorted her to the elevator, she soared inwardly at the happiness she felt whenever she communicated with Donovan. It seemed like they'd known each other forever. She wondered if that was the way of love, falling head-over-heels at first sight. The smart side of her said love was no such thing, but the romantic and lonely side of her encouraged her inner self to put aside the negativity, and to let the love light shine into the dark space that had been in her heart for so long.

Soon they were in the car. The drive to the restaurant took a little longer than usual because of the traffic, but Toni didn't care. She'd cleared the rest of her schedule for the afternoon just in case they ended up doing a bit more than just lunch. They parked in a nearby parking garage and walked briskly to the restaurant, losing themselves in the crowds milling about in the city's bustling downtown business district. Ten minutes later, they were seated in a booth across from each other.

"You okay?" he asked. "You've gone awfully quiet all of a sudden. I hope I didn't say or do anything to make you mad on the way over here."

"No, everything's cool. I'm just a little nervous is all. You know how it is. Or at least I think you do. As I said, I'm not exactly a real pro in the singles game."

Donovan laughed and said, "I realize this is only our second date, but there's nothing to be nervous about. You can say anything to me." He paused as if lost in thought, but she could tell he was just playing for time, most likely hoping she'd calm down. "Uh, would you like a drink to help you relax? I think it might help a lot."

"Yeah, sure. Why the hell not?" she said, growling like a lioness, "I'll have what you're havin'. Bring it on!"

"I always loved that movie," Donovan said. "That Meg Ryan fake orgasm scene is just the best, don't you think? Very realistic!" Donovan slapped the table, palms flat, and in a staged whisper he said, "Yes, yes, yes! Oh, baby! Yes!"

"Hard to believe *When Harry Met Sally* came out eleven years ago already," Toni said. "Hey, I could use a refill." She waved a make-believe empty highball glass under his nose. "Like right now. I'm so thirsty, babe! Oh, I'm just dying of thirst! I'm in a damned desert and I'm lookin' for an oasis! I don't need no dang camel. Just gimme ... *waa ... ter!*"

"Were you always this melodramatic?" he asked.

Then they both laughed in a more relaxed banter.

Donovan gestured to the waitress, who came right over. Toni trusted him enough to order her his preferred drink from his favorite bartender in Atlanta, a guy named Frank who looked like he was a zillion years old. As Toni took in her surroundings, she observed the restaurant wasn't as crowded as she thought it would be. The atmosphere was not trendy or extremely fancy, but undeniably chic. The guests were mainly professionals, some of whom were in booths having conversations while others stood or sat at the bar. She noticed the soft music that played in the background wasn't so loud that she had to raise her voice to be heard. She was also aware of the faintest of hints of Donovan's cologne as the pleasing odors of food wafted from the kitchen.

She smiled at him. "Oh, before I forget, thank you for the lovely bouquet. It made me feel like a queen."

"You are absolutely a queen!" he said, grinning from ear to ear. "Toni, I have to say, there are plenty of beautiful women out there, and you are certainly one of them. But for the type of guy I am, well, uh … how should I put it?"

Donovan paused. "The qualifications I'm looking for in a woman? Well, first off is she's got to be 100 percent down to earth. Just plain and simple good looks and a better brain is what I'm after. I told you that. That's what I see in you. A woman who's smart, witty, independent, and has a strong personality. I just love your electric smile. So, I wanted to express your beauty in the arrangement of the bouquet."

"Why thank you, Donovan," she replied, letting her gaze wander briefly over his face. She got a little thrill from listening to his kind words. *Hmmm, he's truly charming.*

She picked up her glass and took a sip of her drink. It tasted strong. "Whoa! What's in this anyway?"

"Now, if I knew what was in it, it wouldn't be called Frank's surprise. Besides, he won't tell me. He said it's his secret formula."

She raised her eyebrows and chuckled softy. "Well, maybe we better order some food before I get bombed. We wouldn't want that, would we?"

"I bet you're like a tiger when you've got a good buzz on." He faked growled.

Toni blushed. His remark embarrassed her. She wasn't sure why. "Oh, I don't know about that. I'd probably pass out on you if I had more than one of these lady killers," she said, holding up the highball glass and taking one more swallow.

"Let's eat!" Donovan said. He gestured to the waitress again, and she came over and took their orders.

Lunch was cordial, nothing overly personal was discussed. She shied away from mentioning her ongoing trouble with Lorna. Nothing heavy. Just small talk, good food, and one killer drink that had made her feel a little dizzy before the food arrived. When the meal was done, Donovan said he had to get back to work too. They arranged to see each other later in the week. Donovan drove Toni back to the office. He parked in the loading zone in front of the building, got out, and opened the passenger side door for her.

"Now, aren't you quite the gentleman," she said, grabbing her purse as she got out of the car.

"I aim to please," he said.

There was an awkward pause. She wasn't sure what she wanted to say or do. He moved closer to her, then he kissed her softly on the lips. She felt a surge of passion flow through her. She leaned into the kiss a little more, and she felt him tremble. She stood back from him, noticed the satisfaction in Donovan's facial expression.

"Now, that was really nice." he said.

"You could say that again!" Toni said. She laughed, said goodbye, and hurried into the lobby, glancing over her shoulder as she stepped through the entrance. Sure enough, Donovan was still standing there watching her go. Smiling, she walked straight to the elevator. Toni stepped off the elevator and was almost back to her office when she heard a familiar voice coming from the break room. She opened the door, and, much to her surprise, she found Audrey and Lorna in mid-gossip. Lorna smiled warmly when Toni walked in.

"Hey!" Lorna said.

"How'd lunch go?" Audrey asked.

Toni said hello and answered Audrey's question. Then she asked Lorna what she was doing in the office when she said she'd be working from home for the duration of the week.

"Oh, I had some things here that couldn't wait," Lorna said. "Just picking up some case files."

"I see," Toni said. She went to the refrigerator and took out a bottle of water. She twisted off the cap and drank right from the bottle. She leaned her butt against the counter and asked how Lorna was doing with Charles.

"Oh, fine," Lorna said.

Toni sensed she was lying through her teeth.

"Things have been going well between Charles and me. There's a possibility he may be offered a good paying position with a new company in the area. He's on an interview with them right now, and I'm waiting to hear from him. So, I'm killing two birds with one stone. I'm picking up work here, and I'm waiting on my soul mate for some great news!"

"Oh, that's terrific, Lorna!" Audrey said, her voice practically a squeal. "I know how much you guys have been wanting him to land a new position. Maybe things will smooth out between you two if he's back at work."

"That's what I'm hoping for," Lorna said.

Toni saw a look of sadness quickly pass. Lorna may have been putting on a good front, but she couldn't fool either her or Audrey. "Look, since you're here unexpectedly, it would be good for us three to sit down for a quick chat."

"About what?" Lorna asked, sounding wary.

"About the agency. Where it's going," Toni said. "Where we're going. Come on, you two, let's go to my office and have a proper sit down."

Toni led the way out of the break room, and her two partners followed. When they were ensconced in Toni's office, Audrey and Toni sitting on one sofa, and Lorna on the other, Toni said, "As you know, we've been worried about you recently. We know—"

"Okay," Lorna interrupted, waving her hand in the air. "I know where you're going with this. You're gonna tell me I have one foot out the door, and if I don't straighten up the other one will follow. Is that it?"

"Why? Does that surprise you, Lorna?" Toni asked. "I must tell you, I met with Larry Bentley to discuss the possibility of going forward with a dissolution of our partnership with you based on your lack of performance these days. Things have gotten that bad. Bad enough to squawk to a lawyer about things best left on the playground, but Audrey and I felt we had no choice."

Lorna squirmed in her seat and glared at Toni. "You don't really mean that, do you? You actually went behind my back and talked to Larry?"

"We were advised to tell you we'll be giving you three months to get your personal affairs in order," Toni continued, ignoring Lorna's question. "Or, we'll have to consider taking legal action to enforce a buyout under the nonperformance clause in the partnership agreement. We're having a meeting in two weeks with him again to discuss the matter, and to determine the share value with our tax accounting firm just in case things don't work out. In short, Lorna, we're getting all our ducks lined up in a neat little row. We'll be ready to act if we have to. We don't want to fight things out with you tooth and nail, but we will if we have to. We'll definitely act aggressively if you force us into a tight corner in court."

Lorna leaned forward; her attention fixed on Audrey. Toni could almost feel the white-hot rage boiling within her friend. She wondered where the fire was when it came to dealing with Charles. When it came to him, she seemed to be no more solid than Silly Putty.

"So, Miss Audrey, what do you have to say about all this? I bet you're the one who's behind stabbing me in the back after all these years. After all I've been through lately. You should be ashamed of yourself. Really? You call yourself a friend. I don't think so. Not if you want to cut me off at the knees when I'm already down."

Toni thought about stepping in, but she let Audrey keep the floor.

"The truth is we're tired of your nonchalant attitude about what's been going on with the agency. You've been spending less time here, and although we don't want to break up our partnership, Toni and I have been carrying most of the weight," Audrey said, shooting Lorna a sympathetic but firm gaze. "If you don't want to be a part of our organization anymore, there's no reason we can't end this amicably."

Lorna closed her eyes and sighed. She leaned back on the sofa, folded her arms across her chest. "Let me tell you something. Don't think you can kick me to the curb without a fight. I'm going to get *my* lawyer to review our partnership agreement, and I'll hire him to look into the value of the private shares I have with the company as well." She gritted her teeth in silent fury. "I don't trust you two anymore. I think you're both backstabbing lying hypocrites, and I'll keep thinkin' that unless I see something different. Our friendship seems to have come to a bad end, and all because of what? A man. I think that's a cryin' shame. What happened to us? We were sisters once."

"It's not a matter of trust. It's about professionalism. We don't want to find ourselves in a compromising position regarding the company in the near future," Toni said.

Lorna stood up from the couch, taking her purse with her. "I suggest you let me know the date and time of your next meeting, so I'll be sure to be here with my lawyer."

Lorna turned her back on them and stalked out of Toni's office.

"That went well," Audrey said, her sarcasm obvious.

"You think?"

Toni hurried into the conference room ten minutes late. She held a cup of coffee in one hand and several file folders in the other. She placed the folders on the desk, sat down, said hello to Audrey and Alicia, and took a sip of coffee. She cleared her throat and said good morning, thanking her cohorts for rearranging their schedules to attend the meeting. She took a deep breath. "Let's get started. Alicia, I know you've been waiting to know what's happening with the company, especially after having to cover in Lorna's absence. Audrey and I have been stalling because we needed to speak to Larry Bentley before we agreed on any particulars."

Alicia nodded. "Yes, I've been a little confused about the entire situation. I would like to know what's going on."

"And you deserve to know," Audrey said. She told Alicia everything.

"I don't know what to say. This is kind of hard for me. After all the time I've been working with you ladies you've all treated me not only as an employee but as a friend. I mean, I'll be willing to do my part in trying to keep the company afloat so we won't lose any clients. However, I want you to know no matter what the outcome is, I won't be taking anyone's side in this."

"Of course," Toni said, "We respect your decision to remain neutral." She opened a notebook. "Now, let's get to the agenda, shall we?"

Toni spent the next hour or so in the meeting. It was odd, but she didn't really miss Lorna. In fact, the meeting seemed to go much more quickly and smoothly with Alicia taking over for Lorna. As Toni walked quickly back to her office to make some client's calls, she felt sad about the apparent demise of her and Audrey's friendship with their former college roommate. Somehow, life didn't feel like giving Lorna a fair shake of it, and Toni wondered why.

"Girl's done nothin' to nobody," she muttered, shaking her head as she got settled behind her desk. "She deserves a damned lot better than what she's getting."

Toni grinned as she hung up the phone. Donovan's voice still lingered in her ears. He'd just invited her to an African-American music and Arts festival, and she said yes, of course. She glanced up as Audrey knocked on her office door and sat down in the sitting area.

"Hey, Audrey," Toni said. She got up from her desk and sat down next to her best friend.

"Was that Donovan you were talking to?" Audrey asked.

Toni nodded. "How'd you guess?"

"I've noticed ever since you started dating Donovan you've been acting a little giddy lately. It appears you two are hitting it off pretty well."

"I can't explain it. He's so damn sexy and intelligent, and he actually makes me laugh. And the way he looks at me with that twinkle in his eyes … makes my heart skip a beat."

"Oooh, it sounds like somebody is smitten!" Audrey laughed.

Toni got up from the couch and went to the window to look at the view she loved so much. As she observed the panoramic view of the city, even the spring weather seemed to be celebrating. The sun shone brightly, and Toni wanted to stretch out her arms to touch the white puffy clouds as they floated along in a bright blue sky. She blinked a few times, and then turned and re-focused her attention on Audrey, whose statement had caught her off guard.

"Sorry, I spaced out for a moment," she said, sitting back down. "Yeah, I would say I'm in a good place right now. From the moment Donovan and I met, he's been super attentive. The other day he sent me another bouquet of flowers and a thank you card to commemorate our third date. He puts a smile in my heart and a spring in my step. And, get this, on our last date he said he wished we could spend every waking moment together."

"Be careful, girl. He could be a serial stalker," Audrey said with a laugh.

"Really, Audrey?" Toni looked at her in amazement. "We're simply dating. Besides, stalking only happens after you've broken up."

"You know I'm just joking with you. But seriously. It seems to me after all those meals and flowers he's been showering you with he is taking it very seriously. You know what's coming next?"

"What? Sex?"

"Well, as the song goes, if you dance to the music, one day you're going to have to pay it to the piper."

Toni understood once she started dating again there were unscripted rules. Eventually, Donovan might want to take their relationship to another level. But she felt mature enough to deal with whatever came her way. She glanced over at Audrey with a sense of calm and ease.

"I know how to play the game. Besides, who's to say I don't want to sleep with him? Maybe I do. Maybe I don't. But I'm tellin' you, I know you and Lorna are getting it on with your boyfriends like a bunch of rabbits in heat. Why should you guys be the only ones having fun, hooting and hollering all night long? I think it's high time for me to go for it!"

"Why, you nasty little heifer," Audrey laughed as she leaned back against the sofa. "I should have known you'd be trying to get your freak on."

"Damn right! Speaking of getting a freak on, how come I haven't heard any juicy details about you and David lately? You keepin' secrets from me, or what?"

"No way, girl!" Audrey said. She clapped both hands together three times, as if she were summoning a genie from a bottle. "David and I are hot and heavy. You know that. I've told you as much more than once. As a matter of fact, we're going out tomorrow evening to a black-tie affair. It's a fundraiser the senior lawyers at his office sponsor every year."

"Sounds like we're both going to be busy this weekend," Toni said. She thought about Lorna, how the distance between all of them had been growing wider with every passing week. "You know tonight would have been our girl's night out? Like we used to do before Charles came back to screw with Lorna's head. I really miss our hanging out together."

"Yeah, I miss our girl's night out too. Oh, that reminds me as to the reason why I came to see you. I noticed in the database that Lorna has been keeping in touch with her clients."

"I guess she has to do whatever she needs to do, and we'll do whatever we need to do. I'm sure there'll be more drama when we meet with her lawyer. What do you say, let's get out of here early and start our weekend?"

Toni shut down her computer. She picked up her pocketbook, briefcase, and car keys.

Audrey got up from the couch. She raised her right arm in the air and made a fist. "Here's to another fun weekend!"

10

Audrey laid her black satin strapless gown, long white gloves, and seamless black silk stockings on the bed. She smiled, knowing she'd be sexy as hell at the charity gala David had invited her to attend with him. It was the first time she was going to meet David's colleagues, and she intended to dress to impress. She got dressed, and she put on her diamond teardrop earrings and pendant, and then slipped into a pair of three-inch-heel, sling-back black patent-leather pumps. As Audrey stood before the full-length mirror in her bedroom, she smoothed her hands over the fabric of her dress—a nervous habit she often found herself doing. She took a deep breath and slowly exhaled.

This is perfect!

She sat on the bed, anxiously awaiting the call from David that would say he was on his way to her. He hadn't been able to be specific earlier because he had a court appearance. Those, as she knew, could run longer than intended. She glanced at the clock on her nightstand, feeling like she did so every five minutes. Time ticked on. She got up and started pacing.

Well, isn't this great. I'm all dressed up and he doesn't even call to say he'll be late.

She waited another ten minutes, but still no call came in from David. Her worry and anxiety increasing, she dialed David's office number, but the answering machine picked up the call. She left a message: "Hello, David. This is Audrey. I'm patiently waiting for you to pick me up. Remember?

You invited me. If something came up and you're going to be late or you can't go for some reason, please call to let me know."

Her mind started racing as she hung up the phone. *Why isn't he calling me?* She called him two more times, and each time it went to voicemail. *Ugh, where the hell is he?*

She didn't want to seem clingy, or that she was coming on too strong. Heaving a sigh, she reluctantly walked into the living room and over to the bar to pour a glass of merlot. She took a big sip. Rage suddenly seized her.

"Bastard!" she screamed as she threw the half-full wine glass against the wall, and immediately regretted doing so because the glass shattered into a million tiny pieces, staining the carpet with deep red splotches.

Why is this happening to me again? She groaned.

Pure anger bubbled through her veins as she carefully moved back the curtains and gathered up the broken glass before wiping up the carpet with a damp rag. Then she picked up the bottle of wine and sat down on the couch, wondering if she should finish it. She wasn't fond of drinking by herself, but she thought it would help calm her nerves. She drank right from the bottle and kept drinking until she passed out.

Audrey lurched awake. At first, she was disoriented, unsure of where she was for a few seconds, but she quickly realized it was dawn and she was in her living room. She also realized that David had stood her up for some reason, and her anger returned. She tried lifting her head, but it throbbed so hard she couldn't turn too much to the right or the left. She rested back onto the couch. The muscles in her stomach clenched, and her insides contracted. Wincing in pain, tears welled up in her eyes. She tried not to cry. Told herself to suck it up and be brave, but the tears came anyway, and they weren't from just being stood up. They arose from years of loneliness, years of not fitting in like Toni and Lorna did.

She got up from the couch, groaned, and noted she'd fallen asleep on the sofa dressed to the nines in her evening gown and expensive jewelry. The scent of her perfume lingered in the room. She sat there for a few moments trying to figure out whether to wait for David to call her, or should she call him? Not sure what to do, her neck tensed up again.

Feeling drained of energy, she unzipped and removed her dress, and took off her jewelry before heading to the bathroom. A cool shower and two cups of black coffee later, her anger had subsided. Not wanting to wait any longer, she called David. Once again, the call went to voicemail. This time she did not leave a message.

She thought, *Oh my God! Suppose he was involved in a car accident? I could never forgive myself if he was lying hurt in the hospital and I didn't go looking for him.*

She quickly dressed in a pair of black pants and a gray pullover sweater, placed her dreadlocks up in a bun, and put on a little lip gloss and eyeliner. She grabbed her phone, car keys, and purse before heading over to David's apartment. There was little traffic at such an early hour, and if he was at home, she was ready to pounce. She wanted to confront him about his complete lack of consideration on her part. A short time later, Audrey entered the lobby of his fancy building. The concierge greeted her and she signed in. The ride on the elevator to the tenth floor went fast. Once she arrived at his front door, she took a deep breath and rang the doorbell. No answer. She rang again. This time she heard footsteps. An unidentified woman opened the door.

"Can I help you?" the woman asked.

Audrey's eyes widened in shock as she focused on the young female standing in front of her. She was beautiful with a creamy complexion, delicate nose, well-defined cheek bones, and an oval face. Her black hair was unkempt and fell to her shoulders. She looked at least twenty-five-years-old. But what amazed Audrey was the black satin nightgown and robe the woman wore. The thin material clung to her curves, and she had it loosely tied at her waist revealing a full-round belly.

"I - I'm here to see David," Audrey replied.

"Who're you?"

"I'm a legal aide from his office, and I have some urgent papers for him to sign," Audrey lied.

"Just a second." The woman closed the door and Audrey heard her footsteps as she flip-flopped away. Moments later, David came to the door wearing black-and-white striped pajamas. When he saw Audrey, he smiled crookedly, came out in the hallway, and quickly shut the door behind him.

"Hey, what are you doing here?" he asked, rocking back on his heels, his hands in his pajama pockets.

Audrey gritted her teeth and forced a smile. "What do you mean, what am I doing here? The question is what happened to you last night? You freaking stood me up! And who was that Miss-Two-Tons-of-Fun waddling around in her robe like she lives here?"

"I tried calling you several times," he said. "But I lost my cellphone service."

Audrey frowned and held up her right hand. "David, does it look like I was born yesterday? Now I don't know what's going on here, but I need you to tell me the truth."

She stared intently at him, noting he looked awful. He had dark circles under his eyes. It was as if she was seeing him for the first time. Then he shook his head and blew out a breath.

"I'm afraid it's a little complicated," he said. "She's an old acquaintance from my home town in Louisiana. I bumped into her when I visited last Christmas. We became friends again, but we remained strictly platonic as she had a boyfriend at the time." He brought his hand up to brush back his hair. "Anyway, to make a long story short, after they broke up, she relocated here to find a new job and we met up again a few months ago."

"Yeah, well, all that sounds very interesting. So, tell me, is that your baby she's carrying?"

His face screwed up into a mask of discomfort, and it took several seconds for him to speak.

"Yes," he finally said.

Audrey stood there at a loss for words. Her whole body started shaking, and she thought her legs were going to give way. She wanted to slap him so badly. She raised her right arm, brought it back, and was about to let David have it when she stopped in mid-strike. He just stood there looking at her with the saddest expression on his face. She'd never seen him looking so down, and she fought back the urge to mother him, to take him in her arms and protect him from the big bad world.

Honestly, don't even think about it, girl, she thought. *Now you best get the hell outta here, if you know what's good for you.*

"Why in the hell did you do this to me?" she asked, trying to control her anger and grief.

"I'm sorry, Audrey. I was going to tell you," he said. "I just didn't know how. The right moment to tell you just never came up. I kept putting it off. In a way, I think I was in denial."

"That's bullshit, David!" she said. "When were you going to tell me? After you finished using me for sex? How convenient for you. Now that you've knocked up your little girlfriend and can't have sex with her anymore, you mislead me on an online dating site just to get into my panties. You disgust me!"

David looked away.

"Is that how it really went down, David? Am I right to think you're nothing more than a scum bag?"

There was more awkward silence as her question hung in the air. When it became obvious David wasn't going to explain, she rolled her eyes. "Are you kidding me, right now? You aren't going to say anything?" Then she held up both her hands, as if she was trying to stop traffic. "You know what? Just forget it. At this point, I wouldn't believe anything you have to say anyway."

The tears that had welled up in her eyes streamed down her face. Audrey turned away and hurried toward the elevator.

"Audrey, wait! I didn't plan for this to happen."

The elevator doors slid open. Audrey stepped into the car without looking back. She left the building and headed back to her condo. On the way, she couldn't stop thinking about the way he had just treated her. Her temples throbbed, and she could hardly breathe. She pulled over on the shoulder of the road and turned off the car engine. Rocking back and forth, her mouth opened, but there was no sound. In that instant, the memories of all her failed romances resurfaced. This one was by far the harshest.

"Oh, God! How could I have been so stupid," she said and buried her head in both hands. Suddenly, she began to sob. Tears trickled down her face. "Damn you, David!" she screamed, banging the steering wheel with the palms of both hands. She should have known better, especially after hearing stories about men who only trolled the Internet for sex. She should never have let her guard down. Never have trusted. Never have had faith in the honesty and integrity of other human beings, and allowed herself to be so vulnerable.

As the cars whizzed by, she wondered where were they all speeding off to. Were the drivers going home to their families? Or was someone rushing to meet a loved one, only to be jilted like she was? Audrey took a deep breath and exhaled. Looking in the rearview mirror, she noted her face was red and puffy. She dried her eyes with a tissue, rolled the car window down, braced her hands on the steering wheel, pulled out onto the expressway, and hit the gas. The cool breeze blowing in her face made her feel stronger. She gripped the steering wheel hard, and she vowed to never let anyone get close to her again.

11

The alarm clock buzzed on the nightstand next to Toni's bed, jolting her out of a deep sleep. Groaning, she rolled over on her side and turned the clock off. She lay on her bed, the covers pulled up under her chin. Images of her and Donovan making wild, passionate love invaded her thoughts. She blamed the vivid, carnal scenes she saw in her mind's eye on the sex-laced conversations she'd been having with Audrey. Her libido surprised her as her sexual draught grew more desperate. She and the girls had always talked about the three-date-rule, where after three dates you would know if a person is a good match for you, and she felt she and Donovan were connecting. *I am ready for the next level.*

Her date with Donovan to the Black Music and Arts Festival wasn't until later that afternoon, so she had plenty of time to get a manicure and pedicure and maybe buy a new outfit. She willed herself out of bed, took a cool shower and washed her hair. After a light breakfast, she headed out the door. With her hair still damp, the soft waves became more pronounced as they air dried.

At two o'clock sharp, the downstairs bell chimed. *Hmmm, he's always on time. No wonder I like him.*

Toni trotted over to the door and pressed the intercom. When Donovan announced himself, she buzzed him in. She hurried into the bedroom to grab the backpack she'd packed for the festival, pausing to admire herself in the floor-length mirror. She'd tried to keep her look casual and simple.

Her hair was pulled back and tied into a ponytail, which was simplicity in itself. Always something of a clothes horse, she'd found it hard to resist buying her new outfit—a long-sleeved pink floral blouse, black cotton vest, white jeans, and open-toed strappy sandals. And so, she went for it.

She slipped the backpack over her arm, and then hurried to the front foyer to open the door just as Donovan knocked. She answered the door and smiled up at him. He was handsomely dressed in khaki pants, a crisp white shirt, a khaki cap, and Timberland boots. He'd draped a sweater casually over his shoulders.

He tilted his head slightly to the right. Smiling broadly, he said, "Wow! You look terrific!"

"Thanks. I could say the same about you," Toni replied.

Then he touched her chin to tip her face up, leaned in, and gently kissed her. She closed her eyes, and the sensation of the softness of his lips and the moist caress of his breath gave her goose bumps. When they parted, Toni looked deep into his eyes, and blushed. "You see what you do to me?"

"I can't help that you melt in my arms," he said teasingly.

He stood aside as Toni locked up, and then he took her hand and led her to the elevator. They rode the elevator down to the parking garage, and a short time later, Toni sat in the passenger seat of Donovan's Mustang as he sped west on the freeway. It was a beautiful day with temperatures at around eighty degrees. Bright sunshine, a light breeze, and practically zero humidity made conditions quite pleasant for the drive to the festival, and for the experience of watching the bands from the field. It would be a time when Toni could really let her hair down, as it were, and she looked forward to it. She also viewed the coming evening with a touch of anxiety because she wasn't sure just how the night would end.

They arrived at the festival and parked in an open lot, then joined the crowd trudging noisily to the field. A huge crowd had already gathered. Toni stopped to explore several booths featuring local artists and various vendors from Africa and the Caribbean. They all had specific items that represented individual cultures: traditional scarves, paintings, statues, beautiful clothing of woven fabrics, wood carved sculptures, handmade soaps and jewelry. Toni was particularly drawn to the booth with stylish necklaces and gemstones from South Africa.

Perusing and meeting new people, they walked hand-in-hand so as not to lose each other in the crowd. The smells of Southern-style cuisine—fried chicken, sausages and peppers, and greasy hamburgers—made them hungry. They decided to order tacos and glasses of beer. After finishing their meal, they made their way through the crowd to attend a live performance of an eclectic mix of jazz musicians. Time flew by fast. As the sun set over the horizon, a spectacular firework display was the evening's finale that drew loud cheers from the multitude. The night's air, clear and crisp, danced with energy as Donovan wrapped his arms around Toni's waist and pulled her to him. He suggested they get a late supper at a nearby Chinese restaurant, which they did. The restaurant was filled with Asian wall hangings, large ornate Chinese screens, and tastefully decorated antique tables with the glow of red lanterns hanging from above.

"Are you adventurous?" he asked, as the waiter filled their water glasses.

"That depends on what you mean by adventurous," she said.

"Have you ever eaten duck?"

"No."

"Well, may I suggest the Peking duck? It's really delicious."

She smiled and nodded. "Really?"

"Yes, really," Donovan said, flashing her a sexy smile. "It'll melt in your mouth."

"Okay then," Toni said, putting her menu down on the table. "I trust you."

Toni enjoyed trying new things and felt the night was full of promise. They ordered a four-course meal: wonton soup, garden salad, and then she had her first taste of roasted Peking duck served with fried rice and steamed vegetables. Forty-five minutes later, Toni and Donovan were finishing up with their meals.

"So, what's the verdict? Did you like the duck?" he asked.

"Um, yes. I thought it was rather flavorful, a bit sweeter and juicier than chicken."

"Good. I'm glad you liked it," he said, motioning to the waitress. "Would you like to see the dessert menu?"

"Sure. I still have enough room," she said, patting her stomach.

For dessert, they fed each other spoonsful of chocolate chip ice cream with fudge sauce. Then, after reading their fortune cookies, they topped the night off with a glass of dry red wine. Just as they prepared to leave, it started raining.

"Wait here. I'll get the car and bring it around so you don't get wet," Donovan said.

She watched him rush out from under the awning in front of the restaurant and dash across the parking lot. He was her knight in shining armor. She felt giddy, like a little girl on her birthday. Donovan pulled up, she got in, and they headed east back to Atlanta. The rain and wind increased as the sky darkened. Thunder boomed. A fork of white lightning creased the night. Toni sensed the storm was getting closer.

"I don't like this," she said, fighting back her nerves. "Never liked thunderstorms."

"Me neither," Donovan said, keeping his eyes on the road ahead. He slowed down even more when the red taillights of a semi loomed out of the murk. Hail began to beat on the roof. "Jesus!" he said. "Visibility is down to nothing. I tell you what. My place isn't too far from here. Let's hang out there for a while until the storm passes."

"Sounds like a plan," Toni said, relieved they were getting off the freeway. She didn't like the idea of a Mustang tangling with an eighteen-wheeler in the middle of a bad thunderstorm. As the hail continued to pelt the car, Donovan maneuvered cautiously down the side streets until he pulled into his parking spot at the rear of the apartment complex. As they exited the car, he grabbed his car keys and they ran through the downpour into the building.

By the time they reached Donovan's apartment, both were drenched and out of breath. He took out his keys, unlocked the door, and held it open for her to enter. He fumbled around for the light switch then flipped it on, and he helped her off with her backpack "Boy, is this storm something, or what?" she said, taking off her soaked vest and sandals.

"You're tellin' me!"

Just then, a clap of thunder shook the building and the flash of lightning followed almost instantaneously.

"The storm must be right on top of us," Donovan said, padding into the living room to the wet bar. "Drink?"

Toni followed him into the living room. "Yeah, sure! A drink would be nice."

Donovan poured them both glasses of red wine. "Here, this should warm you up. I'll be back in a minute. I'm getting out of these wet clothes. I'll see what I can find for you too while we put your things in the dryer." Then he disappeared around the corner.

Toni stood off to the side sipping the wine, quickly scanning the room to get a sense of who this man was. She observed it was an open layout. The living room was tastefully furnished with a black leather couch and a matching loveseat that went well with the rustic wooden coffee table. A few magazines and books lay on the coffee table. A large plasma television was perfectly placed on the wall across from the couch and loveseat. In the corner sat a tall fiscus silk tree.

Just beyond the living room was a galley kitchen with stainless steel appliances and two high-backed stools around the granite countertop. The adjoining dining area had a soiled plate and a half glass of wine on the round glass top eating table. The apartment, although messy, was by no means dirty.

She smiled. *A typical bachelor's pad.* And then she sneezed.

"You all right?" he called out to her from the bedroom.

"I'm fine. Just feeling a bit chilled is all."

Donovan came back into the living room wearing a white terry cloth bathrobe. He was holding a large bath towel and a long-sleeve white shirt. "Sorry, this is all I have to offer you. I would give you my robe, but it has holes in it. I know you wouldn't appreciate that."

"This will work just fine." She took the towel and the shirt, looked around for the bathroom.

"The bathroom is next to the bedroom on the right," he pointed. "You can toss your clothes out, and I'll take them to the dryer."

"Thanks," she said, and sneezed again as she headed in the direction he pointed. In the bathroom, she peeled off her wet clothes and dried herself off, noting how sexy she looked when she undid her ponytail and let her hair down. She dried her hair with the towel, and then she ran her fingers through her hair to make it look just right. Satisfied, she put on the shirt. It covered her all the way down past her thighs. She picked up her wet clothes and left the bathroom. When Donovan saw her, she was pleased to see he was momentarily speechless. He finally said she looked fabulous, that the wet rain-washed look agreed with her.

"Why, thank you, Donovan! You make me feel all warm and fuzzy inside." She preened in front of him, pushing her right hip out and pouting in what she hoped was a seductive way.

"Here, gimme those," he said, reaching for her wet clothes. "We'll have 'em bone dry in a matter of minutes. And I'm gonna go get changed myself."

She handed him the clothes, and he went to the laundry room that was located in the rear of the apartment. She heard the dryer start.

"Be out in a minute," he shouted from what she imagined was his bedroom. She walked over to the loveseat and sat down very gingerly and crossed her legs. When Donovan came back out, he was wearing worn blue jeans and a T-shirt. He smiled at her and poured more wine. He put a George Benson jazz album on the turntable.

"Oh, I love George Benson!" she squealed, clapping her hands together.

"I had no idea you were into jazz," he said.

"That's all my aunt played in our house. I see you have a vast selection: Miles Davis, Thelonious Monk, John Coltrane ..." She was babbling so fast she hoped he didn't hear the tremor in her voice. He looked so sexy. His T-shirt clung to his muscular chest. The palpable sexual tension in the air made her heart beat faster. Thunder rumbled in the distance.

"My father was the one that got me hooked," Donovan said. "On Sundays when he cleaned his trumpet, he would play along with various artists. I guess it was peaceful to him. You know what they say ... music soothes the savage beast."

"That's why I like listening to jazz. It really relaxes me after a long day at work."

Toni breathed in sharply through her nose as Donovan moved toward her, closing the distance between them.

He cleared his throat and asked, "May I have this dance?"

A smile crossed her lips, and he took the glass from her and placed it on the coffee table. Donovan reached down and took her by the right hand, gently pulling her to her feet. He put one hand on her back and held her close, and then he wrapped his other hand around her waist. They two-stepped in an unhurried, sensual way. Breathing in his fresh scent, Toni closed her eyes, allowing the melodious lyrics of the song to overtake her.

Feeling good in his embrace, she rested her head on his chest, listening to his strong heartbeat, which was as rapid as her own.

Then, their dancing slowed down a bit, and Donovan brought his hand to her face, and she could feel his warm breath on her skin as his lips claimed her mouth. Toni wrapped her arms around his neck and shamelessly returned his kiss, glorifying in the feel of his tongue parting her lips, and then plunging into her mouth.

At that moment, Donovan broke off their kiss, and he bent down to pick her up. Cradling her in his arms, he carried her over to the couch and gently laid her down. In the softness of the light, he unbuttoned her shirt and draped it over her shoulders. He gazed down at her with an expression that made her heart flutter.

"I've been dreaming of this moment," he said, his voice thick with emotion and passion.

He started kissing the softness of her neck, then suddenly stopped, and asked, "Are you okay with this?"

Tilting her head back, she laughed. "Of course, I am!"

"Then come with me," he said, standing up.

Taking Toni's hand, he led her down the hallway to his bedroom. As they entered the darkened room, he turned on a lamp by the bed.

"I want to see all of you," he said, removing her shirt.

"Well, here I am," she whispered, gripping the bottom edge of his T-shirt and lifting it up.

Following her lead, Donovan reached behind him and pulled the T-shirt the rest of the way off. Toni drank in the sight of his muscular chest and six-pack abs. She knew he worked out in the gym, and now she saw the results. She really liked what she was seeing. Toni's face felt hot and flushed, and she couldn't speak. Her hand roamed lightly over Donovan's chest and down to his abdomen, causing him to tremble. She unzipped his pants, pulled them down, revealing his arousal beneath his boxer shorts.

Oh, God, this is going to be well worth it.

Donovan slipped out of his pants and underwear. "Come," he said, taking her right hand and leading her to the bed. He hovered next to her, pulling her close to him. His kisses, hot and wet on her neck and collarbone, sent shivers racing down Toni's body. He knew all the right spots to touch, caress, and kiss. "You taste so good. I could eat you up," he said.

"Oh, so you want to turn me into an appetizer now?" she whispered.

"That's not a bad idea," he said."

She closed her eyes and arched her head back as he planted more kisses from her breasts down to her stomach, and repeated his actions at a lower altitude. Toni felt the effects of his passionate lovemaking all the way down to the tips of her toes, relishing every moan he brought out of her. When he came up for air, he perched himself on his elbows. "You're so beautiful," he said. "You know that, don't you?"

"Oh, I guess I can get by on a good day," she said. "But thanks for saying so."

Donovan flipped onto his back, and Toni took him on a journey of body and mind. She rained kisses down his neck to his abdomen, and then she went lower. A few short moments of passion later, Toni couldn't wait much longer to have him completely, and Donovan obviously felt the same way.

"Take me," Toni said. "I want you to take me right now!"

Donovan obliged, and time seemed to stop.

Later, Toni stirred and glanced over at the digital clock on the nightstand. It was nearly three o'clock in the morning. She shifted slightly, and, in doing so, awakened Donovan. He moved closer and threw one leg over hers. Sensing his arousal, they resumed their lovemaking.

12

Lorna huddled in bed in the fetal position with her knees pulled up close to her chest. Her lower lip throbbed, and her teeth hurt, especially on the right side of her jaw. She hoped Charles hadn't done any real damage to her this time. She knew on an instinctual level that he might really hurt her one day, but all she could feel at the moment was numb. She couldn't bear to think about the future. Thinking about and enduring the present was already too much for her to take. She cringed when she heard the bedroom door open.

"Honey," Charles said, his voice soft and gentle, the opposite of what it had been just a short time ago when he had screamed at her, calling her the most awful names. When he'd hit her with a closed right fist, she knew the situation had escalated quite possibly beyond whatever control she exerted, or hoped to exert. If he was willing to punch her in the face, he might be capable of going much more off the deep end. The very thought of that scared the hell out of her, but she still felt paralyzed, feeling almost like a prehistoric fly frozen forever in time in the stony balm of solid amber.

"Honey, did you call the police? If you did, don't worry. I won't be mad at you. I just want to know if you ratted me out. Come on, babe. You can tell me the truth."

She rolled over on her other side to face him. "No," she said, stifling a sob. "I didn't call the cops this time, but I damned well should've." She buried her face in her pillow and started to cry.

"Well, two cops are here. They want to talk to you."

Lorna wondered who'd called the cops, but she didn't have to think far or wide. All the neighbors knew they were the screaming dysfunctional couple.

"Why?"

"What do you think?" Charles hissed, leaning close to her. "Some asshole probably heard us fighting and called it in. Come on, let's go. Fix yourself up and get out there. They can't be here. Not on any account. I don't want cops anywhere near here."

Lorna panicked. If someone called the police, then Charles would go crazy when they left, unless she told a good story. Charles could actually blame her for everything, and then start beating on her again. Trembling with fear, she got up and walked into the bathroom. She did her best to freshen up, and then she went into living room. Two cops stood just inside the door. Both were big. Both could put Charles down in a minute, and that somehow made Lorna feel a tad more confident. Just then, Lorna thought about saying something to piss Charles off to get him to freak out in front of the cops. Who knew? Maybe he would possibly lose his cool, assault the cops, and end up in county lockup.

"I'm Lorna Stanley," she said, offering the white cop her hand. "What can I do for you?"

The two officers identified themselves. The one named Todd said, "We got a complaint about a loud argument. A neighbor heard crashing sounds and breaking glass."

"So what?" Lorna asked, putting both hands on her hips. "Couples fight all the time. It's no big deal.

"How'd you get a fat lip?" the other cop asked.

"I bumped into a door."

Lorna could tell neither cop believed a word of what she was saying.

"A door, eh? You sure?" Todd asked.

"Yeah, I'm sure," Lorna said, glancing over at Charles.

"And you are?" Todd asked Charles.

"Charles. Charles Hunter. I'm Lorna's boyfriend."

Officer Todd scribbled in his notepad. "Would you mind if we speak with Ms. Stanley alone for a few minutes?"

Lorna could see that the request annoyed Charles, but he had the good sense to not give the cops any guff. He nodded and stalked into the kitchen. "I'll be right here if you need me, honey," he said, glancing over his shoulder at Lorna.

Lorna ignored him.

"May we sit down for a minute?" Todd asked.

Lorna gestured toward the couch. "I guess so, but I don't understand what this is all about."

Officer Todd and Lorna sat down, while the other officer stood nearby.

"We think your boyfriend gave you that fat lip," the other cop said. "You know, we can protect you if you file assault charges against him. You have options. You may feel trapped in your abusive relationship, but you're really not trapped. Only if you make it so. It just feels like you're in a cage and can't get out. The reality is the only cage you got is the one you built for yourself."

Lorna felt nothing but despair and shame. The policeman was right. She did have options, and she wondered why she didn't pursue any of them. She wondered why the miserable status quo remained acceptable to her, despite the pain, fear, and shame.

"Did Mr. Hunter hit you?" Todd asked.

Lorna shook her head. "No."

"Domestic abuse is a crime, you know," Todd continued. "But we can't do a thing unless you press charges. If you don't act, then you're setting yourself up for a pretty dangerous situation. Abusers generally get worse over time. You could end up in the hospital, or worse."

Lorna said nothing. Her head was spinning. All she wanted was to be left alone. She wanted to crawl into bed and never get out.

"Are there any firearms on the premises?" Todd asked.

Lorna shook her head.

"Any children live here?"

Lorna said no. Then she stood up and crossed her arms over her chest and glared at the officers. "I think you should leave now."

Both officers just looked at her. The one named Todd looked disappointed.

"Okay, Ms. Stanley, have it your way," Todd said. "Think about what I said, okay? You don't have to live like this. We're here if you need us. All you have to do is call." Officer Todd took a card out of his right breast pocket. Handing her the card he said, "If you need anything at all, you just give us a call."

Lorna took the card, dropped it on the coffee table, and walked to the door and opened it. Both officers said goodbye and left. She sat back down on the sofa, praying Charles would stay in the kitchen a little longer.

13

Toni jerked awake from a deep sleep. The first thing she noticed was a large abstract painting on the wall beside her—some sort of monstrosity named the "Ruby Diffuse," a smear of reds, oranges, and pinks against deep blue slashes spangled with tiny white stars. She heard someone snoring. It took a moment to recall exactly where she was. She rolled over and saw Donovan lying on his back next to her. Save for the thin white flannel sheet that covered his bottom half, his rock-hard torso was exposed. She sat up on her elbows admiring the definition of his chest and abdomen going up and down, and all she could concentrate on was the heat and passion they created the night before.

I must have really exhausted him, she thought.

Quietly getting out of Donovan's bed with a big smile on her face, she went into the living room to collect her clothes, and then made her way to the bathroom. There was a tube of toothpaste in the medicine cabinet, but since she had no toothbrush, she improvised by placing the paste on her right index finger and rubbing it over her teeth and tongue. There was no way she was going to face Donovan with stinky morning breath, and her tongue felt really gross. Gazing at her reflection in the mirror, she attempted to tame her unkempt hair, achieved a bit of a victory, and called it quits.

She decided to take a quick shower to refresh herself before getting dressed. She stepped inside, turned on the tap, and let the hot water cleanse her. She turned her head up to let the jets spray directly on her face, reviving her and making her feel tingly through her very core. She laughed softy as she lathered up, realizing it had been so long since she'd had sex her body was sore in places, she almost forgot existed. She leaned against the wall of the shower and closed her eyes, enjoying the relaxing steam as she caught a whiff of Donovan's musk oil that still lingered in the bathroom.

Donovan had aroused emotions in her she truly had never experienced before. His lovemaking was gentle, and he was not afraid to display his affection in a variety of ways. She could not remember the last time she'd gotten her blood pumping like that, but she had no regrets. Besides, she was way overdue for some fun in the sack, especially after being so preoccupied at work, and with all the trash stuff going down with Lorna.

By the time Toni was dressed and ready to leave, Donovan still slept on. His black hair poked in tufts from his head. The expression on his face was priceless, a thin smile drawn across his lips. Toni sat on the edge of the bed and stroked his chest hairs gently, letting her fingers curl around them. Then she leaned over to kiss his lips. He opened his eyes.

"Good morning, beautiful," he said with a grin.

"Morning."

"Where you off to so soon?" he asked, as he propped himself up on his right elbow.

"I have a lot of paper work to catch up on, but I wanted to tell you I had the most delightful evening."

Donovan reached over and squeezed her hand.

"No, *we* had the most delightful evening. Why don't you wait up? I'll get dressed and take you home. Better yet … I can take you out for some breakfast. How does I-Hop sound?"

"Sorry, I already called a cab. It'll be here any minute."

"Are you sure you don't want to stick around a little longer?" he rolled over, exposing his bottom half, and winked. "I'll make it worth your while."

Toni looked at him for a moment, remembering with affection the heat of their lovemaking just hours earlier. Finally, she muttered, "You have no idea how tempting that sounds, but I have to go." She bent down and gave him a quick peck on the lips. "I'll call you later."

"Okay," he said. "Make sure the door locks behind you, and have a nice day!"

"Oh, you bet I will. Have a nice day, I mean. How could I not after last night?" she said. She laughed when he turned over in a fetal position with his hands tucked under his cheek, and playfully pretended to snore. "Yeah, you're just such a big ol' baby," she said.

Fake snore.

"Uh-huh!" she said, and walked out of the bedroom.

Toni left Donovan's apartment, and the taxi took her back to her condo. She greeted the doorman with a brief but friendly nod, and hurried to the elevator. Up on the tenth floor, she hurried to her door, rushing to unlock the door as she heard the phone ringing off the hook. Without removing her backpack, she hurriedly answered the call before it went to voicemail. It was Audrey. She said she wanted to come over, she was feeling depressed. Although Toni wasn't in the mood to act as therapist or cheerleader at that moment, she invited Audrey to come right over, if she liked.

"Okay. See you in a few," Audrey said, and hung up the phone.

Toni walked into her bedroom and changed into a pair of blue jeans and a black silk blouse. She put on her slippers and went into the kitchen to make a pot of coffee. A half hour later, Audrey arrived with warm croissants she had picked up from the bakery on the corner. They sat side by side at the kitchen table sipping coffee and eating their croissants.

"So, what happened that you couldn't talk about over the phone?" Toni asked.

Audrey set her croissant down after taking a bite. "Remember I told you David invited me to his company's annual dance?"

"Yes, I remember. How did it turn out?"

"Well, he stood me up! And he didn't even call to tell me what happened. I tried calling his cell phone and his office number and it kept going to voicemail. So, this morning, I got this bright idea to go over to his house, you know, to see if he was alright.

I thought maybe he was in a car accident or something."

Toni was afraid of what she was going to hear next, but decided to ask anyway.

"What happened when you showed up at his apartment?"

Audrey's eyes became watery, and then she closed them. "I'm so embarrassed. I don't believe I didn't see the red flags. From day one, it was right there in front of my face." She paused. "That son of a bitch has a girlfriend, and she's pregnant. I'm the other woman! Can you believe that? I got played so friggin' bad I just want to slap myself upside my own head for being such a damned idiot. How could I have been so stupid?"

Toni was surprised. David had seemed to be the ideal online dating candidate, or at least that was how it seemed at first. Obviously, there was more to David than met the eye, and she suddenly wondered if the same thing could be said of Donovan. Pushing her concerns about her own new online boyfriend from the forefront of her mind, she concentrated on Audrey. "What do you mean he has a pregnant girlfriend? How did you find out?"

Audrey stood up and began pacing. "The bitch answered his door. I told her a fib that I was from his office and I came for him to sign some legal papers. She goes to get him, and he comes to the door in his friggin' pajamas looking like he just woke up."

She tapped the palm of her right hand against her forehead. "I'm so stupid."

Toni paused, seeing how distressed Audrey had become. "Oh, Audrey, I'm so sorry for the way things turned out. But you're not stupid. How could you have known? Unless you're a mind reader, you'll never know what's in a man's head. I think most men think with their little heads anyway. You know that."

Toni laughed ruefully, shook her head. She was pleased her last comment at least got Audrey to smile, albeit only for a flash.

"Looking back, this relationship was always on his terms," Audrey said. She wiped a tear from her eye. "I really thought I found the right one. As it turns out, he was just a lying, cheating, selfish bastard!" she sniffled. "I can't believe this! I'm giving up on men altogether. I think I'll just live the rest of my life as an old maid with cats."

"Oh, come on, Red. Don't be silly!" Toni stood up and walked over to Audrey's side, putting her hand on her shoulder. "Of course, you're going to date again. Take a good look at you. You're a beautiful, talented, educated woman. Any good man would be lucky to have you. You just have to figure out what you want in a man, and then choose men with those attributes."

She paused for a moment. "I know I may sound like a hypocrite right now, but hear me out. Look, if it wasn't for you, I wouldn't have joined the dating website and met Donovan. But maybe you need to stay off the website for a while and focus on yourself. You haven't had time to do personal work on yourself in order to build a stable foundation for love. If you take the time to step back and build yourself up, I'm sure the right man will come along eventually, particularly if you're actively out there beating the bushes from a place of emotional security."

Audrey looked at Toni. "Are you seriously trying to get me to look at the bright side of things right now?"

"Yes! When it all gets down to it, all you got is you. Remember to look at the world not from a selfish perspective, not from a totally all-me attitude, but from a healthy standpoint of self-preservation and self-interest. If a relationship won't give you what you want, then get out of it. It sounds to me like your relationship with David might have been hot in terms of sex, but it was built entirely on sand. And high tide was a comin'!"

"You think love is transactional, don't you?" Audrey asked. She sighed and sat back down at the kitchen table. Toni followed suit. "Yes. I think love shouldn't be about what you get. It should be about what you give."

Toni thought for a long moment. She felt her friend's pain. Hell, she'd had enough pain on her own to fill several eighteen-wheelers. She knew Audrey had long suffered from failed relationships with men, and, truth be told, she thought Audrey brought many of the problems on herself. Still, that didn't mean she deserved to be constantly abused by indifferent, selfish, men.

"Everything in life is transactional. Wish it weren't true, but wishing doesn't change the way the world is. So, you want love, you got to play the game. You want to play the game, you got to pay to play. No one thing in this entire thing we call life is free. No free lunch, baby! So, of course love is transactional, just like everything else. The trick is to come out on the winning end of the equation. The trick is not to get totally screwed in the process."

Audrey rubbed her eyes and shook her head.

"Things are going to be a little rough for a while. Naturally, you're upset about what David did to you, but you'll see in time everything will work out," Toni said. "In fact, he may have actually done you a favor by tipping his hand the way he did. If he hadn't stood you up, how would you have ever known he was playing you? The answer is you wouldn't know. And that's what they're all counting on. They play you for a fool, and then they run away as fast as their little rabbit feet will carry them."

Audrey nodded slowly, with a pained expression on her face, then said. "Damn it, Toni. I hate it when you're always right."

They hugged.

"Thanks, Toni, for being such a good listener. Lately, I've been feeling like I don't know who I am. I knew I could count on you to help me sort this out."

As they pulled apart, Toni locked eyes with Audrey. "Hey, that's what we have each other for. Hell, sometimes I don't know who I am either. I think we're just sisters in search of ourselves." Then she added, "I have an idea!"

"What?" Audrey asked.

"What do you say we go catch that new matinee movie, and then have a slice of pizza and a glass of wine to end the evening. My treat!"

"Okay. Cool. If you're treating, let's go," Audrey said. "I could really use a distraction about now."

Toni gathered her pocketbook and car keys, put back on her shoes, and they linked arm in arm as they laughed on the way out the door.

14

The weather in late April brought with it the first definite waves of summer humidity from the Gulf of Mexico. The crisp cool Canadian highs had receded, as always, and everyone on the streets of Atlanta seemed to be wearing shorts already. Lorna was dressed in a light blue skirt, a pale pink blouse, and black flats she'd specifically chosen in case she was forced to stand on her feet for a long time in the courthouse. As she sat in her car in the lot near city hall, she thought about the enormity of what had happened in just the space of a day or two.

After the cops had showed up, Charles went crazy, as she predicted. He stormed out of the condo, but not before cuffing her around a bit more just to make his point. She'd screamed at him to get out and never come back. It was then she made up her mind to file a restraining order against him. If he roughed her up again, she'd press charges. That was the plan, and now she was following through with it. She got out of the car, grabbed her purse, and hurried into the courthouse. The process of filing the restraining order was a hassle, but she got through it. For Lorna, taking such a firm step meant she was on her way to a new life. For starters, she changed the locks on the front door.

Taking action emboldened Lorna, made her feel like she was in control. She knew Charles was a bad apple, that he'd show up in her life again, despite the restraining order, but she'd shown him she was no pushover. She had enough inner strength to stand up for herself when the chips were down. And, a few days later, Charles did show up. She called 9-1-1 right away, and the cops arrested him with practically no questions asked. Unfortunately, the judge released Charles on his own recognizance, meaning he was still out on the street and posed a potential threat to Lorna. Although she knew it was stupid, she still felt like his absence in her life left a giant hole that could never be filled again. She hid in her condo, spending most of her time in bed in a deep depression, a depression made all the deeper after she discovered Charles had been stealing money from her.

Now, several days later, the cops were scheduled to come by with Charles so he could get his belongings. She'd wanted to throw everything out into the dumpster in the alley next to her building, but she knew better than that. Part of her still loved Charles, and part of her still feared him. She didn't want to provoke him in any way. She wasn't keen about seeing him, but it couldn't be helped. She applied some light makeup and lipstick, slipped on a simple black maxi dress, and complemented it with a string of pearls and clip-on earrings. She reached for her bottle of Chanel No. 5 perfume, carefully unscrewed the stopper, and gently dabbed the scent behind her ears, on each wrist, and to the back of each knee. It was Charles's personal favorite.

At that moment, the doorbell rang. She made her way to the door, and her hand trembled as she turned the door knob. A police officer stood there with Charles next to him. Charles greeted her with his brightest smile, and then he started licking his lips, looking deranged. She stood tall.

"My, my," Charles said. "you're looking mighty sexy. Were you going somewhere?"

"Maybe."

The cop spoke. "Good afternoon, Ms. Stanley. I'm officer James Prescott. We're here to pick up Mr. Hunter's things."

She stepped aside and pointed to a large trash bag by the door. The officer told Charles to pick up the bag.

Charles peeked into the bag, and then looked at her. "Where's my other stuff?"

"What other stuff?" Lorna asked.

"My suits, shoes, jewelry, and cologne."

She paused for a moment before responding. "I'm sorry, but I bought you those items. So, they'll stay here with me."

"Why are you doing this to me, Lorna.? Why are you being so cruel?" he asked.

Her eyes narrowed. "Cruel! I'm being cruel? After what you did to me?" She turned to the officer and said, "You see, not only did he beat my ass, but he stole my money too."

"I haven't stolen jack shit from you!" Charles said, his voice low and menacing.

Lorna stepped forward and got in his face. "Yes, you did steal my money, you jerk! And I want it back."

"Okay, calm down, Ms. Stanley," Officer Prescott said, stepping further into the condo. "How much money did he allegedly steal from you?"

"I'm missing about ten thousand dollars. Only I know I can't press charges against him for stealing from me because the money was in a joint account. So," she wagged a finger under his nose, "you got away with it this time, but some day, somehow, you're gonna get what's comin' to you. And I wanna be standin' right there when you go down."

"Come on, Mr. Hunter, your time is up. You're not to engage with Ms. Stanley under any circumstances." The officer turned to Lorna and said, "Thanks, Ms. Stanley, for letting us come get his stuff. Have a nice day!"

As they continued to walk down the hallway, she heard Charles blurt out, "But what am I supposed to do about my suits? I need them for job interviews."

"I'm afraid you two will have to settle this in court." the officer responded.

Charles turned back toward Lorna still standing in the doorway. "Well, sweetheart, I guess I'll see you in court!"

Lorna closed the door quietly behind her and wearily leaned against it. She was exhausted beyond measure, and yet images of Charles appeared in her mind. Her feelings for him were too much to ignore, despite all that had happened. She was so angry with herself for being so ambivalent she was unsure just how to react. However, she refused to shed another tear over him. More than anything, as she watched parts of her life unraveling, she felt the discomfort of having to face the uncertainty of her future alone.

Lorna was running late for the staff meeting, a gathering between her and her partners about the future management organization of the company. Or, in short, it was a meeting to decide whether she would continue to be part of the agency. She tried to get out of the confrontation by saying she wasn't feeling well, which was technically true. Ever since the altercation between her and Charles she'd been suffering from headaches, upset stomach, and it had been hard for her to sleep. But Toni was persistent.

As she stepped off the elevator, she heard voices coming from the conference room. She'd called earlier and told the receptionist to let Toni know she was on her way. She counted to twenty and took a deep breath before opening the door. Toni, Audrey, and Alicia were already seated at the table with their yellow legal pads, fancy fountain pens, and steaming mugs of coffee. Their conversation ended abruptly when she entered.

Audrey looked up, pushing her glasses atop her fiery red hair. "Well, look what the cat dragged in," she said. She stood up, came around from behind the conference table, and gave Lorna a big hug. Giving her a peck on the cheek, she then stepped back and said, "You surely are a sight for sore eyes." She turned to Toni. "Isn't that right?"

Toni followed Audrey's lead. "You got that right, sister!" she said. "We've missed you around here. We were sorry to hear about your police trouble with Charles. We understand things have been crazy for you."

"Way crazy. You don't know the half of it," Lorna replied. She put on a cool façade as she took a seat and put her tote bag on the floor beside her. Just then, Larry Bentley strolled into the room with a cup of coffee in his hand. "Good morning everyone," he said, taking a seat to the right of Toni. They exchanged brief small talk before Toni brought the meeting to order.

"Weren't you suppose to have your lawyer here as well?" Toni asked Lorna.

Lorna felt empty inside, as if she'd lost her only connection to the larger world outside of her own tortured existence. She wanted desperately to have everything go back to the way it was before Charles reentered her life and set about destroying it little by little, but she knew it was impossible. "This isn't easy for me," she began. "I cancelled having my lawyer here because there's been a change of plans."

The girls looked at each other and then at Larry.

"What kind of changes are we talking about, Lorna?" Larry asked, taking a sip of his coffee.

Lorna turned to the other ladies, who were watching her intently. Then, with a sad, misty-eyed stare, she muttered, "I'm asking for a second chance. I want to continue working with you guys."

Toni stood up and ambled over to the side table to pour a glass of water from the pitcher. Audrey shifted slightly in her seat, and Alicia took a quick sip from her cup.

"I realize I've let you guys down lately," Lorna said, summoning the courage to continue. "I know I've missed time. Alicia, I know I've pushed work off to you when you were already busy. I get it. And I have no excuse other than to tell you Charles has put me through sheer hell these past several months."

"We know," Toni said. "It's terrific to hear he's no longer in your life."

"Yeah. I packed him up and kicked him to the curb," Lorna said. She tried to sound cheerful and confident, but she still felt so bad just thinking about Charles hurt a lot.

"What is this really about Lorna?" Toni asked.

Lorna tried to make eye contact with everyone. "I'm saying I made a terrible mistake, and I know I've been performing below expectations. I want to say I'm sorry I let you down, and to please give me another chance to reconcile our partnership."

Audrey laughed, somewhat derisively in Lorna's view.

"Are you listening to what you're saying? Imagine how we're feeling right now after what you did. How do we know if we can ever trust you again?" Audrey asked.

Lorna thought for a moment, and said, "Why wouldn't you trust me? We've been friends since college. You guys know me. You mean to tell me no one in this room ever did something they've regretted?"

Toni crossed her arms. "I think we all make mistakes," she said.

"Agreed," Audrey said. "Nobody's perfect. What you say is all well and good, but I'm sorry, Lorna. I just don't believe you—"

"How can you say that?" Lorna said, not giving Audrey a chance to finish. "I understand how you might feel angry over what happened, but you've got to give me a chance. I hardly have any money left in my savings because Charles cleaned me out. My credit is shot to hell, and now I stand to lose my car and my condo."

Lorna forced back her tears. She took a tissue from her purse and dabbed her eyes, being careful not to mess up her makeup.

"Look," Toni began, holding up her hands in a form of surrender. She turned to face Lorna. "When you agreed on joining in this partnership, I assumed it meant we had the same goals. Now, if your goals have changed, just let us know. We won't judge you. The consensus right now is we buy you out and be done with it."

Lorna pressed the palm of her hand against her forehead as she felt an oncoming headache forming. "I'm sorry for all the chaos I may have caused. But I'm willing to show you ladies I've gotten myself together and I'm on the right path for the company."

During the whole ordeal Alicia had remained silent. Finally, she spoke up. "Ladies, I think we ought to give her another chance. She seems really remorseful, and is at least willing to be honest with us."

Toni sighed. "I don't know if this is a good idea, but if you all are willing, we can discuss this further."

"Yes, why don't you ladies do that," Larry said. "Give it a few days to weigh the pros and cons of whether it's best to continue with this partnership, or to write her a check and move on. The last thing you want to do is make a rash decision that will lead to regrets."

Larry stood up, and put on his hat. "It's not worth stressing over any particulars right now. Call me when you've come to a decision, and I'll have the proper papers drawn up." He then grabbed his briefcase and left the room.

Audrey opened her mouth to say something, but remained silent when Toni raised her hand.

"Okay, Lorna. Why don't you give us a few days," Toni said, "and we'll get back to you with our final decision."

Lorna nodded. "I understand." Then she jumped to her feet, snatching the tote bag from the floor. Offering a weak smile, she left the conference room without saying another word.

15

Toni leaned back in her chair and patted her mouth lightly with the napkin. She gazed around her at the other diners, most of whom were well dressed professionals from the downtown business district. Giovanni's was one of the classiest Italian restaurants in town. Donovan had made a good selection when he suggested taking her there. She'd just finished a delicious meal of spaghetti and meatballs, garlic bread, and a garden salad, along with a bottle of red wine.

Donovan reached across the table and took Toni's hand in his. "A penny for your thoughts."

Toni shook her head. "I'm sorry. I spaced out for a moment. I guess I'm still thinking about our meeting with Lorna today. I hope whatever decision we make will be the right one."

"I'm sure you'll come up with what's in the best interests of both Lorna and the company." He gently squeezed her hand.

"Thanks for lending me your ears. I really appreciate it." She looked at him and smiled, wondering how much more of him there was still to discover. She wanted to get to know more of him. "You know what? You look kinda cute when you arch your eyebrows like that."

He cleared his throat. "I believe that's too much wine talking. Would you like to order some dessert?"

"Oh, no! I'm stuffed and ready to go home."

After paying the bill, they left the restaurant. Donovan drove her back to her condo. He rode with her to the tenth floor and accompanied her to her door. Donovan leaned in, putting his arms around her waist and pulling her close. He kissed her gently on the lips.

"Thanks again," she said.

"It was my pleasure. Night now." He turned to leave, and Toni quickly grabbed his right arm.

"Hey, what's the rush? Why don't you come in. I could brew us some coffee."

"Oh, okay. That would be nice," he responded without hesitation.

Toni opened the door and he followed her in. The living room was dark. She turned on the lamp next to the couch, and he sat down. Toni placed her purse and keys on the credenza and kicked off her heels.

"Just give me a few," she called over her shoulder as she walked to the kitchen.

Minutes later, Toni reappeared carrying a tray with two coffee mugs, sugar, and cream. She had the biggest smile on her face as she knew Donovan was leaving on a business trip the next day, and she was trying to figure out how to spend their last few hours together. The soft light from the lamp created a sensual glow in the room.

Donovan's eyes followed her as she knelt, placing the tray on the table. Toni smiled, and relaxed next to him on the couch.

Donovan took a sip of his coffee. "You know, I'm glad I got a chance to hang out with you tonight because I've been thinking a lot about us lately. And …"

Toni directed her feet towards him, allowing her right leg to roam up and down his leg. She rested her head against his chest. He brushed her hair back and gently kissed her forehead. Toni stood up. He pulled her down into his lap as she straddled him. Leaning forward, she explored his mouth with a long fluid kiss. He tasted of wine and desire.

With the roundness of her hips pressed against him, Donovan shifted his body, and he managed to pull the wrap-around dress she wore over her head. Then he ran his hands up her back and unsnapped her bra. Toni shivered as his hands glided over her naked skin. Time seemed to stop as they concentrated on probing each other's mouth.

When at last they parted, Toni looked directly into his eyes and said, "I think it's time we undressed you."

Donovan wrapped his arms around Toni's waist, securing her body against his, and eased himself off the couch, lifting her up. Toni enveloped her legs and arms tightly around him as he carried her into the bedroom, placing her on the edge of the bed. She unbuttoned his shirt and eased him out of it. Tugging at his belt, his pants fell to the floor, and they both tumbled back onto the bed, laughing. Donovan draped one arm around her back to hold her while raising her shoulders slightly off the bed. He leaned in and pressed his lips to hers. She kissed him back.

"I just love your sensual kisses," she breathed.

With his lips pressed against her ear, he whispered, "I love yours too!"

Donovan hungrily claimed her mouth again, and she gasped. After several minutes of intense lovemaking, their bodies shook in the grips of an orgasmic release. Satiated, they both fell asleep in each other arms.

The alarm clock went off at five. Toni jolted awoke. She reached over and turned off the alarm. Donovan opened his eyes. Yawning, he leaned forward and kissed her forehead.

"Morning baby," he said, his voice soft and warm.

"Morning sunshine," she said, roaming her hand over his chest and neck.

Donovan smiled at her. Pushing the blanket aside, he sat up sluggishly. "I would love to go another round with you, but I'll surely miss my plane if we do."

"I know, babe," Toni said. "What I got last night ought to hold me until you get back. You were really great, Donovan. I have to tell you."

She noted the self-satisfied smug grin that flashed across his face. For a few seconds, the look bothered her. It seemed somehow wrong, out of place, it revealed another facet of her man she hadn't often seen.

Donovan headed to the bathroom to shower. There was no time for a conversation or breakfast. He needed to go home and pick up his suitcase to catch a flight to California for a very important business meeting.

After he dressed, he walked over to where Toni lay in bed.

"Thanks for a great send off." He knelt down beside her and kissed the top of her head. "I'll call you later."

"Okay," she said, groggily. "But we really never got a chance to finish our conversation about what you were thinking of us."

"Well, I'm afraid it's gonna have to wait until I get back. Now go back to sleep."

Once Donovan was out the door, Toni closed her eyes as she relived the previous night's moments, and shivered over Donovan's touches. A sudden tide of joy leapt out of her heart. She didn't want to seem too needy or desperate, but after years of tearing her hair out over unhealthy relationships, she recognized she was falling hard for Donovan. She couldn't wait for his return from his trip so she could tell him.

16

Audrey stared out the window at the view from the conference room trying not to show Toni how really annoyed she truly was at the terms of Lorna's newly drafted contract. Larry Bentley had just left, and so had Lorna. Audrey had thought of speaking up earlier, but Toni seemed intent on enacting the new terms, and so she didn't say a word. Now she regretted her silence. She swiveled around in her chair to face Toni.

"What's this? Whatever Lorna wants, Lorna gets? Between us, I told you we should have agreed to buy back her shares and let her go. I'm sure that money would've helped her out until she found another job."

Toni raised her eyebrows. "I'm not sure what the problem is with you, Audrey. Suppose she didn't get another job right away. She could have lost her condo and her car. Would you want that on your conscience? We've been friends with Lorna for years. We should cut her some slack, even though she's been a pain in the ass lately. Besides, what if you found yourself in the same boat one day. I'm sure you would've wanted us to consider taking you back."

"Yeah, but it leaves a bitter taste in my mouth. I just hope she doesn't stab us in the back again. I sincerely hope she got rid of that scumbag boyfriend of hers. Because I'm telling you, if she's lying, and I so much as see them all lovey-dovey as a couple again, I'm moving on. You can count me out on this whole damned entrepreneurial venture."

Toni ran her hand through her hair. "I think we should table this conversation for now. I don't want either of us saying something we'll regret and can't take back."

Audrey nodded. "Yeah, let's. No sense in beating a dead horse."

Just then, the conference phone buzzed, and Toni hit the intercom button.

"Yes, Betty."

"I see your meeting is over. Donovan is calling long distance. Would you like to take his call or shall I take a message?" Betty's voice crackled over the speakerphone.

"Put him on hold and give me three minutes to get to my office, and then you can transfer the call."

"Okay. Will do, Toni."

Toni touched Audrey's shoulders. "I don't want you to feel like I'm dismissing you. Let's just leave things the way they are for now, and we'll talk some more later, okay? Let's just give us all some room to breathe."

Audrey nodded. But when Toni left the conference room, Audrey frowned and folded her arms across her chest. She knew the problems weren't solved, not by a long shot. In fact, Audrey sensed the presence of darkness in their lives, a presence that had not been there before. The changes were relatively recent, and she wondered what had triggered them.

After a restless night, Audrey awoke to the sound of the phone ringing. When she checked the clock on the nightstand, it was 8 a.m. She sat up in bed, stretched, and yawned. Who could be calling her so early on a Saturday morning? She groaned when she saw the caller ID indicated David was calling. She pressed the palm of her hand to her mouth in total dismay. He'd actually had the audacity to call her. The phone rang a fourth time and she quickly picked up.

"We need to talk," David said without preamble.

A big part of her wanted to hang up on him, but another big part of her didn't. She felt deeply conflicted. "Um, what exactly do you want?"

"Look, Audrey, I really need to see you. I could be over in about an hour, and we'll talk then. I don't want to go into anything over the phone."

"I really don't see any reason for us to talk at all, David. I haven't heard from you since I found out about your little fling. Now you're telling me we need to talk? Please! Why don't you just go rot in hell, okay?"

He didn't say anything for a long moment, and then she heard a distinct sigh. "I'd really like to see you. I'll be over in an hour."

Audrey was about to respond, but David hung up before she could. She held the receiver in her hand and listened to the dial tone for a second or two before hanging up. She put on some music and paced around her condo with her thoughts solely focused on David. Should she give him a second chance? Did she really still love him, or was it just a sexual attraction? She wasn't sure, and she wanted to find out. She was pretty sure he was on his way over, and, about an hour later, she was proven right. The intercom buzzed downstairs. She buzzed him in, and then in a couple minutes her doorbell rang. Audrey stood at the door, her heart beating wildly. Now she'd made the decision to see him, she couldn't back down. She took a deep breath before slowly opening the door. As soon as she caught David's eye, he straightened up.

"Okay, so, tell me what do you have to say?" she asked, her hand still holding onto the doorknob.

"Can I at least come in? I want to have a civilized conversation with you," he said.

Audrey peeked out the door, glancing up and down before saying. "Yeah. Come on in. I don't need to have my business all in the hallway."

She stepped aside, and he entered the suite. She sat down in the loveseat across from the sectional. He sat across from her. An awkward silence ensued until Audrey broke it.

"Get to the point, David," Audrey said. "You're not welcome here. Get on with it, and then get out."

She noted David looked sad, as if she'd just hurt his feelings, and she felt a pang of guilt. She wanted to kick herself for feeling like that, for feeling anything for the monster David truly was. But was he really a monster? Or was he merely a flawed human being like everyone else? "Why'd you string me along when you knew you had a pregnant girlfriend? Tell me why!"

"First of all, like I told you, I never planned for any of this to happen. She came by my apartment crying one night, and feeling suicidal after she found her best friend and her man in bed together. In the process of comforting her, well, uh, one thing led to another."

"You actually expect me to believe that's the way it went down? I want the truth, David. No more bullshit!"

David took a deep breath. "You're right. It does sound crazy. That's why I wanted to come over and talk with you face to face." He paused. "Remember when we just had a couple dates, and I told you my sister was in town and she needed some money so I couldn't hang out with you that weekend?"

Audrey didn't respond, and stared at him waiting for him to continue.

"Well, that was the weekend she came over. She was very despondent and talking about killing herself, so I let her stay in my apartment for a week until she calmed down. Then she went back to him, until she realized she was expecting." His shoulders drooped. "Baby, I swear, I never meant to hurt you. It's killing me to see what I've done to you."

Audrey's eyes widened. "How many times did you have sex with her?"

He shook his head. "Oh, my God, you said you wanted the truth. That was the only time."

Audrey fought the twisted emotions stirring up inside her. Blinking back tears, she continued, "So, if she was supposedly living with her boyfriend, how do you know this kid she's carrying is yours?"

David closed his eyes for a moment. "Oh, I thought about that already. She told me there was no way it was her boyfriend's child because he had gotten a vasectomy years ago. But I'm planning on getting a paternity test anyway. Just to be sure."

Audrey felt the grief wash over her. Seeing David made her realize how much she missed him, how much she in fact did love him, despite his flaws and foibles. Despite the fact she knew deep down in her heart she could never trust him completely again. His deceit had permanently sullied the relationship. Intellectually, she knew it was over, but not so emotionally. She didn't object when he got up and knelt in front of her, taking both her hands in his.

"I wish there was a simple solution to this problem. I have to live with this every single day. But I want to do the right thing if the kid is mine."

"So, what do you plan on doing? Marrying her?" Audrey snapped.

"No way! I don't love her. I hate to say it, but I wish it was you having my baby, not her."

"At this point it's not going to help either of us to hear you say that," she said.

"I want you to know what you mean to me. That's the main reason why I came over."

"What are you talking about?" she asked.

"Audrey, I was really starting to fall for you."

She shook her head in disbelief, and looked into his eyes. "Well, it's pretty clear you and I are over."

David reached up and began gently stroking the side of her face.

Audrey caught her breath. His touch was warm on her skin. It sent a ripple throughout her body.

"Stop it, David! You have a lot of responsibilities now, so don't come over here talking about you wanting to be with me … because I'm not feeling it! You hear me! I'm not feeling it!" she lied.

He sighed deeply. "Audrey, I love you! I want you to know that."

Audrey said nothing. She just stared him down.

"Did you hear me?" he asked.

"Yeah, I heard you!" she said. "I mean all of this is new to me. While I've been here thinking about you, looking forward to spending time together, you're over there with your baby's mama doing Lord knows what."

"Listen to me," he said, pulling his hand away, "it's not like that. I've been completely happy with the way things were between us. Besides, she's aware I'm dating you. The only reason why I'm letting her stay at my place is because she has nowhere to go." He stood up and held out his hand. "I want you Audrey, and I wish things could be more solid between us."

Audrey forced a smile. "Yeah, yeah," she said, waving him away with a dismissal. "I think you should leave now."

David hesitated a moment before answering. "Okay. If that's what you want."

He bent down and kissed the top of her head. As she inhaled the scent of his cologne, it brought back so much familiarity. Her body stiffened.

"Please, David, just go!"

"Could you at least walk me to the door?"

He reached down and gently helped her to her feet, and his whole body pressed against hers. He embraced her. Audrey pushed back against his chest.

"What am I supposed to do, Audrey? I still desire you."

"This just doesn't feel right, David. You really need to leave," she said looking down at the floor.

"Damn it, Audrey. I've made it pretty clear it's you I want. Ten days is a long time being without you. Why can't we continue dating, and see where it takes us?"

"Not happening! If we get back together now, I'll feel like you're just using me for sex. I don't want to feel that way, and yet it'll always be in the back of my mind. I'll always wonder if you're cheating on me."

David's pained expression pleased her.

"I don't want to make you to feel that way." He turned away from her and walked to the door. He stopped in the foyer. "I know I've ruined what we had, and I'm sorry. Very sorry. I came over here hoping we might be able to work things out, but it seems not. Can I at least kiss you goodbye?" he asked.

Audrey wasn't certain why, but she agreed before she could stop herself. Trailing a hand up her neck, he brushed a strand of hair behind her ear, and then leaned in to capture her lips in a fiery kiss. One hand slid down the small of her back and the other claimed her waist. In an instant, he held her against the wall. Audrey trembled with unbridled desire. She gave way to the waves of passion breaking over her. His hand came to rest on her stomach as he began to untie the ribbon holding her robe together. Audrey let out a small moan. "David. No." But she knew it did not sound entirely convincing.

David pulled away and he placed a soft kiss on her lips.

"What are you trying to do? Seduce me into submission?" she said breathlessly.

"I want to make love to you so badly it's killing me. I can make all the bad memories go away if you'd let me," he said, running his fingers delicately over her now exposed body. "Baby, please, tell me you want me too."

A shiver went through Audrey's body and she gasped. "I *hate* you David for teasing me like this."

"I never tease," he murmured. "I'll be crazy to let you go." He breathed heavily as his hands continued to roam her body.

Her voice grew softer. "If anything were to—"

"I need you just as much as you need me." He lifted her chin up with his index finger, forcing her to look into his eyes. "You do love me, don't you?"

Audrey stared at him, biting her lip, and then nodded with a smile.

"I love you too," he whispered.

Then he hugged her tight, and Audrey went willingly into his arms. Her body weakened as their kiss deepened. Before her legs gave out, David picked her up and carried her into the bedroom, just as he had done so many times before. She buried her face against his chest, breathing him in, forgetting about time and place and circumstances.

Giving in to each other's needs and pleasures, they attempted to recapture the sense of joy they once shared. Feeling his sculptured body against hers, it made her skin tingle everywhere he touched. Their warm bodies melded together. Audrey felt unguarded allowing David back in her arms, but it felt so right. Besides, the one good thing that came out of it was all her built-up sexual tension would be gone the next day.

17

As a gusty wind rattled the windows of Lorna's condo, she remained in bed listening to the sound of the rain. She was tempted to rest there all day, unwilling to face the world that mirrored her dreary mood. But she needed to get ready for work. She swung her legs over the side of the bed, and walked in a drowsy protest toward the kitchen to turn on the coffee pot.

After all the turmoil Lorna had endured with Charles, she thanked God to have freed herself from his hold. Nonetheless, every time she checked her cell phone, there were text messages and voicemails from him. Although she had read his texts and played back his messages, his words of endearment were hard to interpret. Regrettably, realizing his declarations did not offer anything but false expectations, she deleted them all.

For the first time in a long time, Lorna felt the solitude of her former life. But being alone in her condo didn't feel real somehow. Although it was clean and airy, at times it felt as if the walls were closing in on her. Lorna had put a vase of flowers and candles on her dining room table to cheer her up. Whenever a wave of sadness crashed on the rocky shores of what had become her life, she found herself fluctuating between fighting the feelings of anxiety and depression and giving in to see a therapist as her friends had suggested.

As she gazed at her reflection in the full-length mirror in the corner of her bedroom, everything about her appeared to be the same—her short curly hair, her slender figure, her ample curves. But her eyes were different.

They seemed dark, almost as if a part of her was fading away. Toni and Audrey tried to help, but they were both caught up in their own busy lives. The tension between the three of them had diminished after their recent contract renegotiations. Lorna didn't want to ruin things with her continued feelings of loneliness and despair. At work, she put on a good front, but inside she still churned with a mix of emotions she'd never encountered in the same way.

Riffling through her underwear drawer, she purposefully chose a black pair of silky panties and bra, and sheer black stockings. Then she selected a black tailored suit and black shoes from the closet. The black attire symbolized the state of mourning she was in due to the loss of her relationship. Charles had often said he hated it when she wore nothing but black, and she'd given in. She'd bought clothes with soft colors. Now she was pretty much back to wearing black all the time.

After she finished getting dressed, she went back to the kitchen, poured a cup of coffee, and sat at the kitchen table in quiet contemplation. The apartment seemed so empty without Charles there.

Maybe I should buy a dog, she thought, but dismissed the idea. Dogs were like babies. They required a ton of work, and she simply didn't have time for distractions. The wall-mounted phone rang. She got up from the table and picked up the phone. Charles was on the line.

"You're violating the restraining order just by calling me. If I report you, you'll be in big trouble," Lorna said.

"I was just sitting here thinking about making sweet love to you, honey. I know saying I'm sorry is not enough because I've been doing the same things over and over again. You didn't deserve to be hurt like that, but I've since had a huge wake up call. I'm not that guy anymore. I'm getting the help I need for my anger issues." He paused briefly. "Look, I'm not going to lie to you, I miss you badly, and all I have to say is I'm sorry. I don't expect you to take me back, but can we at least be friends?"

"You're right. We did care about each other, and that's history. I'm glad, of course, you're getting the help you need, but please don't call me anymore."

There was a long pause on the phone, and then Charles said, "You know what? You're absolutely incredible!"

"What the hell are you talking about?" she asked, twirling the phone cord in her right hand.

"I can tell from the tone of your voice you still love me, and I'm dying inside without you. All I'm asking is that you think about what I just said. Why don't you let me take you out to dinner and a movie? I want to prove to you I'm a changed man."

Lorna leaned against the kitchen island to keep her knees from buckling. She wanted to scream. She knew she should hang up, and yet she was still listening to him. Why did she let him exert so much power over her? She still wasn't sure where that submissive quality was coming from.

"Charles," she said calmly, "don't call me anymore, and don't even try to come over here, or I swear you're gonna be sorry. You'll end up in county lockup for sure. You hear me? You don't wanna mess around with me on this."

Lorna hung up the phone, feeling the first stabbing pain of a migraine coming on. She opened a kitchen cabinet and took two of the yellow capsules her doctor had prescribed her for pain. She put on her spring jacket, and drove to work. Upon arriving at the office, she noticed Betty, the receptionist, wasn't at her desk. Heading down the hallway to her office, she saw that Toni and Audrey weren't in their offices either. She was glad neither of them were there, as she wasn't ready to answer any questions. She figured her best friends would see she'd been crying, and they'd want to know why.

Closing her office door, she walked over to the window and opened the blinds. Although the view of the Atlanta skyline wasn't as spectacular as Toni's, it was still quite impressive. She lingered by the window, her spirits about as low as they could go. Resigned to the fact she was going to feel sad all day, and her damned headache wouldn't go away, she sat down at her desk. Her first task of the morning was to place a conference call to one of her largest accounts, a book publishing company. She collected what she needed for the call, went to the break room to get coffee and a buttered roll, and hurried to the conference room.

Lorna had been back at work for two weeks or so, and she'd since realized just how important her position at the agency was in terms of bolstering her own sense of self, her own perception of her very identity, who she was as a woman and a marketing professional. Somehow, all her troubles with Charles had rendered her impotent in many ways that had adversely affected her ability to serve her clients. Toni and Audrey had been right, she had to finally admit, about wanting her to up her game or get out. A drag on the agency's bottom line would threaten the future of the business and the jobs of everyone who counted on the three of them to keep bringing in top clients that could afford to pay fat fees.

Lorna sat down at the head of the conference table. She was early for the call to begin, so she reviewed her notes. The publishing company wanted to launch a new imprint for children's books, and they were about ready to ramp up on the initial marketing plan. If the client went for it, the marketing program could bring in some seriously big bucks. As she studied her notes, she had the creepy notion she was being watched. She glanced up toward the door, and froze.

"W-What the hell are you doing here, Charles?" she asked, standing up from behind the conference table.

Charles glanced behind him, as if he was afraid someone would hear him. He said, "You hung up on me. I didn't like that."

"You better get out of here right now," Lorna said. "Or I'll call the cops on you so fast your head'll spin like a God damned top!"

Lorna noticed that his speech was slurred. She didn't have to go near him to know he reeked of booze. He was probably high on something else as well. She realized with a momentarily surge of adrenalin she was alone in the suite of offices. Her stomach heaved in revulsion she'd ever let him touch her, let alone that she'd been stupid enough to fall in love with him for a second time, the first being when they were in college together. Nevertheless, he did seem strangely vulnerable at the moment. She, despite her anger at herself, still cared about him in a strange sort of way she didn't understand.

Charles closed the conference room door.

"Just what in the hell do you think you're doing?" Lorna asked, feeling the rage inside her start to rise. A trickle of sweat ran down her back. Her heartrate increased. She'd seen Charles when he was at his worst, and he did not seem to be far from the bottom as he staggered slightly when he sat down at the conference table. Lorna sat down too.

"I need you to listen to me without any interruptions," he mumbled.

"And why should I listen to a word you have to say? You're breaking the law just by being here." She removed her cell phone from her purse. "All I have to do is call 9-1-1, and you're toast. You know that?"

Charles smiled and shook his head. "You're not callin' the cops on me. Not today. Now, hear me out."

Lorna knew she should just call the police and get it over with. She knew she was a sucker for even listening for as long as she already had. Yet she said nothing as he began to give a long rambling speech saying how he had come far in his therapy sessions in a very short time, and he wanted her back in his life.

"We could even get married, if you want to," he said.

"That's never gonna happen," Lorna said.

Charles bowed his head. "Listen, I know I treated you wrong. I know I may have worn a mask to prevent people from seeing how insecure I was. Even the so-called perfect person has something to hide. But I've tried everything I could to make you love me. When we hooked up again, I wanted to make you so proud of me. After my luck started to run out and you kicked me to the curb, I felt like a total failure." He looked up at her in a gaze with a worried expression. "I need to know. Do you still love me?"

Lorna hesitated for a moment. "You'll always have a special place in my heart."

"But do you still love me?"

Lorna heard voices and footsteps in the hallway. Alicia opened the door and stepped into the conference room.

"Is everything okay?" she asked. She nodded at Charles, put both hands on her hips.

"Everything's under control," Lorna said, "but thanks for asking. I'm sort of in the middle of something right now, so would you please reschedule my conference call?"

Alicia, still looking puzzled, said she would. She left the conference room, closing the door behind her.

Suddenly, Charles started sobbing softly. "I love you so much, Lorna … don't leave me. I'm so sorry. I'll be good. I promise!"

Lorna leaned forward and touched his arm. "Charles, please don't do this. I wish we could've worked things out. Let's not drag this thing out any longer. Once you get yourself together, I'm sure you'll find someone else."

He waved away her hand. "You don't get it, do you? I don't want anyone else. I want to have a life with you!"

"Like I said. That's never gonna happen. It's over, Charles. Well and truly over. Now I think you'd better leave. Right this very minute!"

Charles jumped up, and in seconds he was on her. He grabbed her arms, forcing her to stand.

"Charles," she yelled. "You're hurting me." She noticed his eyes were as dark as coal.

"If I can't have you, then no one can! Now, come on, let's go!" He proceeded to pull her behind him toward the door.

"Let me go right now, or I'll have your sorry ass arrested again."

"You shouldn't have said that," he said, his voice akin to a low growl.

Before she realized what was happening, Charles had her by the throat.

"What are you doing?" she said, starting to choke, her fear on the rise. She brought her hands up trying to dig her fingers in the soft flesh of his inner wrists to free herself. Charles's eyes bulged as he tightened his grip.

"Bitch!" he snapped. "You made the choice to leave me. Now you're gonna have to suffer the consequences."

Feeling pressure against her windpipe, Lorna closed her eyes and the feeling of complete submission washed over her like a wave. Part of her wanted to give up, and a part of her wanted him to dominate her, to make her feel as small inside as she often did. And, then, the anger returned tenfold. She summoned all her strength, and gave Charles a roundhouse punch in the nose that stopped him cold. He released her immediately.

"What the hell?" he asked, the surprised look on his face making Lorna even angrier.

Blood poured down his face onto his shirt.

"You fuckin' hit me!"

Coughing and gagging for air, Lorna ran for the door. As momentarily stunned as Charles may have been, he was still fast. He was on her in second. "You think you can run?" he shouted, throwing her down on the floor. She hit her head and saw stars. For a split second, she wondered if he was going to actually kill her.

"Now you're gonna pay, bitch!"

Just then, the door to the conference room flew open. Nothing was said. It all happened so fast. Scotty Walker rushed in and put Charles in a choke hold in a matter of seconds. Now it was Charles who couldn't breathe. Toni and Audrey were right behind him and they helped Lorna to her feet.

"Your ass is mine," Scotty said, roughly forcing Charles against the wall with the help of two of his men. He cuffed Charles. "Cops are on their way, jackass." He turned to Lorna. "You okay?"

"I will be. Thanks."

"How'd he get up here in the first place?" Toni asked, giving Scotty a hard stare.

"That's a good question."

"I let him up," one of the guards said. "He showed his ID and said he had business with Lorna Stanley. I signed him in."

"You didn't check the red flag list," Scotty said. "This guy has a restraining order out on him."

The guard looked away; said he was sorry.

"I'll deal with you later," Scotty said.

Lorna leaned against the conference table. Toni and Audrey both hugged her, told her everything would be okay. A moment later, two uniformed officers hurried in. Scotty explained what happened.

"I saw him attacking her," Scotty said. "Who knows what would've happened if we didn't get here in time?"

After hearing from Scotty, Lorna, and the others, one of the cops told Charles he was under arrest for violating a restraining order, assault and battery, and criminal trespassing. "You'll need to come down to the station to make a formal complaint," the officer said to Lorna. Lorna said she would be down later in the afternoon.

"This is all a setup!" Charles yelled, straining against the two cops as they perp-walked him out of the conference room. "You hear me! I'm innocent!"

Lorna sagged into a chair as she watched the cops escort Charles out of the conference room. She couldn't remember a time when she ever felt so low.

18

Audrey relaxed on her couch with a glass of Merlot, and thought sexy things about David. The black lace teddy and matching robe he'd given her added to her lust. They'd made passionate love the previous evening, and she frankly was interested in a repeat performance.

Maybe my handsome man's available for a booty call, she thought with a smile.

She called his cellphone and it rang six times before it went to voicemail. So, she tried texting him. Five minutes passed, and she didn't receive a response. She called his cell again, and again it went straight to voicemail.

Where the hell is he? He said he didn't have to work late tonight.

Then a sense of impending doom overcame her. She felt as though something extremely bad was going to happen about the future of their relationship. Audrey closed her eyes and pictured David out on a date with his supposed ex-girlfriend. Some men, she knew, liked to have their cake and eat it too. She wondered if David was being true to her, then she felt bad about mistrusting him. Yet thoughts of David cheating on her with other women played on her imagination. She told herself she was being irrational, but he was the one who neglected to mention his ex-girlfriend was in town, she'd been homeless, she was having his baby, and that he'd invited her to move in with him until she got on her feet. That was a bit much for even Audrey to take.

I'm a woman, and I know how other women think. I bet she's using this baby to try to win him back.

She called David again. This time the phone rang four times before he finally answered.

"Hello?"

"Hey, there! You okay?" she asked, trying to remain calm.

There was a brief pause. "Yeah. Why'd you ask?"

"Well, I was feeling a little hot and bothered tonight, and I was wondering if you could come over?"

Another brief pause. "Listen, babe, this is a bad time. I'm at the hospital with Sheila. Can I call you back?"

He sounded frustrated.

"At the hospital? What's the matter? Did she go into labor?"

"No, she's not in labor. But I really can't talk to you right now."

"Oh, okay," Audrey said. She could feel the bile rising in her throat. "Just remember that I need you too."

"Audrey," he said slowly, "I'll come by tomorrow after work."

"What about tonight?"

"I gotta go. I'll call you back later."

"Why don't you—"

The phone beeped off.

"Just forget it."

Audrey sighed and turned off her phone.

Am I being a jerk? she wondered. She figured it was possible. Their renewed relationship seemed to be going fine. The sex was great. He was attentive to her. He sent her flowers and bought her gifts. She told herself everything was fine, and that she was being paranoid and should give him the benefit of the doubt. Yet reason didn't prevail over the seed of jealous and suspicion that had blossomed within her. Just how bad things would get she didn't know. She poured another glass of merlot to drown her sorrows, and as the hours ticked on her anger at him and at herself steadily increased until she drifted off to sleep.

Audrey jolted awake, and for a moment she forgot where she was, she'd fallen asleep on the couch. The annoying buzz of the intercom forced her to get up, put on her robe, go to the door, and press the talk button. She noted the clock on the mantel indicated it was seven in the morning. She'd have to get going soon or she'd be late for work.

"Who is it?" she asked.

"Audrey, it's me. David. Can I come up?"

She buzzed him in. David was at her door a couple minutes later. He looked slightly disheveled in his jeans, T-shirt, sneakers, and well-worn leather jacket.

"What's going on?" she asked.

"I tried calling you earlier, but I assumed you turned your phone off," David said, stepping into the foyer. He took her in his arms and kissed her softly. She closed the door behind him, and stepped back, putting some distance between them.

"So, you wanna tell me what's going on?" she asked, pulling her robe tighter around her waist.

He loudly exhaled and shook his head. He started pacing, and Audrey just watched him with her arms folded in front of her. "You wouldn't believe the shit I went through last night," he said. "When I came home from work, Sheila was doubled over the kitchen sink throwing up. I took her to the hospital because we were afraid she might be losing the baby."

Audrey cocked her head to the side, her interest piqued. David stopped pacing and faced her.

"Anyway, the doctor told her it was a stomach virus. He gave her something to stop the nausea and vomiting, and he put her on a bland diet for a week while she recuperates. Needless to say, it was a relief for the both of us."

Audrey took a slight step back, unable to find the right words. Then she spoke, waving her hand in the space between them. "You know what … I'm sorry."

"Sorry? Sorry for what?"

"I've been thinking there's a chance Sheila may still have feelings for you, and if she does, I don't think I can continue in this relationship any longer."

"Oh, for God's sake, baby! You know I don't love her. I love you! You know that, or at least I hope you do."

He gently touched her face, brushing over her lips with his fingertips. "Audrey, we belong together. That's why I'm here to let you know how much I need you in my life. I sensed you were upset last night, and I wanted to make sure everything is okay between us. Now, it seems I was right to see you this morning."

"Sometimes I'm okay with her in your life, and sometimes I'm not," she said. "It's obvious I feel threatened by her. I can see now as time goes by she's gonna need you for more than emotional support, and where does that leave us? Besides, she's having your kid. You're gonna want the child in your life, and that means she's always gonna be hanging around in the background."

"You're right. The child will be in my life. Our lives, if you'll allow it. But that doesn't mean we can't be together. It just makes things a little more complicated, but I'm asking you to be patient with me. I'm asking you to have faith in me, and in us."

"I think you're kidding yourself," she said. She glanced at the clock on the mantel, saw it was getting late. "Things will change between us after the baby comes. You'll be spending more time with her, and you'll neglect me. It's already started."

He took a deep breath, and let it out slowly. "Look, Audrey, yes, she's gonna need my help for a while," he said. "But love-wise? You're the only one for me. I have an idea. Why don't you come by the apartment tomorrow evening after work, and I'll introduce you to her? I want you to get to the point where you feel comfortable around one another."

"I really don't know if that's even appropriate," Audrey said. "Why would she ever want to get to know me?"

"Frankly, she probably doesn't, but she'll do it for me. And, once she meets you, you both might come to a mutual understanding that could smooth everything out. I have several court proceedings today, so I'll be out of the office all day. Why don't you think about it? And, I'll call you later."

Audrey nodded. "If we can find common ground, I think that would be good," she said.

David pulled her close, pillowing her head on his chest. He brushed his lips against her ear and whispered, "I want you to know this wasn't part of my original plan. But with some effort, everything will work out for the best."

His hand moved up to her neck, and as she leaned back to kiss him the feel of his soft lips against hers both riled and pacified her. She gazed up at him, her heart beginning to flutter. "I'm definitely going to take all you just said into consideration," she said.

Then he turned away, and Audrey walked him to the door. As she stood in the doorway for a moment, she waved before closing it behind her. She took a deep breath and wrapped her arms around herself, holding the bitterness inside her. She wanted to believe him with every fiber of her being. But deep down she was sure this woman would mess everything up, and that made her feel sad more than anything else.

19

Toni lay in bed blissfully on the edge of consciousness. The alarm had just awakened her, and she was trying to motivate herself to get up. The phone on the nightstand next to her bed rang, and she was thrilled to hear Donovan's voice when she answered the call. The conversation was short. She hadn't seen Donovan in a while since he'd been traveling on business. She missed him, and told him so. She decided to take the day off.

After they hung up, Toni's heart beat wildly. She closed her eyes and replayed her memories of passionate lovemaking, their bodies sweaty and reeking of sex. Yes, she certainly had missed him, and he'd be at her condo in about an hour. Pushing away her lustful thoughts, she was suddenly highly motivated to get up. She took a nice long shower. She pinned up her hair, and put on a pair of loose gray sweatpants, an oversized shirt, and slouch socks. Then she looked at herself in the full-length mirror behind the bedroom door, and chuckled.

I may not look the part of the girly-girl he's used to, but I'm sure he'll enjoy the new me.

An hour later when the doorbell rang, Toni practically skipped to open the door.

"Donovan!"

Donovan's face lit up, displaying his famous ear-to-ear smile. "Babe, I'm so happy to see you!" he said, pulling her in to wrap his arms around her.

He took hold of her chin and tilted her head up. She rose up on her toes, closed her eyes, and lifted her face to him. As his tongue flickered between her lips, his mouth devoured hers. She could feel the rapid beat of his heart, and taste the sweetness of his mouth.

When they parted, he placed both hands on her shoulders and looked deeply into her eyes. "I'm sorry I didn't call you last night, but my plane landed a little late. I hope you don't mind my calling you so early, and then inviting myself over."

"Are you kidding me? Get your fine ass in here," she said, closing the door behind him. She gazed at him for a long moment. He looked positively dreamy.

"Tell me what's on your mind little one," he teased, running his hand along her cheek.

"You know exactly what I'm thinking," she said, her voice low and sultry. "You're looking good enough to eat. It's been the longest two weeks. I really missed you. I mean I *really* missed you!"

"Would you like to show me just how much?"

"I should say so!" Toni said. She held his hand as they strode into the living room. She wanted to lead him straight to the bedroom. Instead, she figured she'd play it cool and make him wait just a little longer to fan his pent-up passion, so she asked him if he'd like scrambled eggs, bacon, toast, and coffee for breakfast.

He gave her a funny look. "Breakfast? I thought we'd catch up in the bedroom first."

"Okay. Come on, big boy!"

And they did. Their lovemaking was quick and passionate, almost animalistic. Minutes later, lying next to him felt like the most natural thing in the world, as if they'd been soul mates for all eternity. She felt full, and she didn't want it to ever end. Suddenly, in a flash, her mood swung in the opposite direction. She didn't understand why, but she somehow thought her emotions were leading her into potential trouble instead of joy. The feeling of wariness vanished almost as quickly as it had come, and she pushed the negativity out of her mind.

"That was awesome," she whispered. She played with some of the hairs on his chest.

"You were awesome too," he said. His stomach growled.

Toni laughed. "Oh, oh, sounds like somebody's hungry."

"Famished. I haven't eaten anything since late yesterday."

She got up, put on her robe. He got up, put on his boxer shorts, but nothing else. She watched him pad across the room to pick up the jacket she'd thrown in the corner as they ripped each other's clothes off, just like in the movies. He reached into one of the pockets and pulled out a square box meticulously wrapped in shiny red paper.

"I have a little something for you, sweetie," he said, handing her the box.

Toni took the box, unwrapped it, and then slowly removed the lid. Inside was a heart-shaped diamond necklace. She gasped. "Oh, Donovan, this is beautiful!"

Donovan placed the necklace around her neck, and smiled proudly. "The minute I saw it in the window, I knew it was you."

"I love it." She reached up to hug him again, and when their lips touched, their kiss deepened. He ended with a firm suck on her bottom lip.

"Hmmm, please don't stop," she moaned.

"Oh, don't you worry. Trust me. There's plenty more where that came from!"

His stomach growled again. Toni laughed.

"Come on," he said, "let's eat!" He steered her toward the kitchen, playfully swatting her butt.

Donovan helped Toni make breakfast. When everything was ready, they sat down to eat. Taking a forkful of scrambled egg, Toni swallowed and sipped her coffee. "You know, Charles got arrested for assault, among other things. Right in the office, of all places."

He raised an eyebrow in surprise. "Really? What happened?"

She told Donovan everything. "It was real scary. The guy went nuts on Lorna. Just way friggin' nutso!"

"Dude belongs in jail, man! You don't hit women. Every guy knows that."

"Yeah, but not all of them play by the rules. Charles sure didn't. Lorna says he always said he was sorry after he hit her, and she'd go for it. She says it makes her feel weak even talking about it, and I told her talking about it would do just the opposite. It would empower her to break out of the pattern of abuse."

Donovan dabbed his mouth with his napkin. "That was downright profound, Toni! What did she say?"

"She told me she'd take care of Charles once and for all."

"Ooooh, sounds ominous," Donovan said.

"I think she's just talkin' trash," Toni said, getting up from the table.

Donovan got up from the table and picked up his plate. "That was delicious. Thank you, babe."

"Don't mention it. Thank you for the necklace. It's more valuable than a few eggs."

He laughed. "You got that right! Anyway, is Lorna doing better now that Charles is in jail?"

Toni nodded. "Uh-huh. She's in therapy, which is a good thing."

"Sounds like she could use someone to talk to."

Toni said she thought so too as she cleared the table. She loaded the dishwasher, and then they both adjourned to the living room.

"So, tell me," Toni said, "how was your trip?" She sat down on the couch. Donovan sat down beside her. "You mentioned meeting with some very important people."

She'd been wondering how his trip out to Silicon Valley had gone. He'd met with the head of Rockville Center, an information technology company that employed well over two hundred top coders. Donovan's skill set fit perfectly with the company's mission. She'd seen how excited he'd been to be called out there for an interview. In fact, he had seemed almost too excited.

"It was a pretty eventful meeting." Donovan inched closer to Toni and took her hand in his. He spread out her fingers and began playing with them.

Toni suddenly felt uneasy, as if the other shoe was about to drop.

"As I told you, the company had been sitting on my resume for almost two years before the head of HR contacted me to see if I might be interested in a top-tier position as a Software Developer at their San Francisco headquarters."

"So, how did it go? What did they say?"

Donovan squirmed in his seat.

"The guy who runs the IT department officially made me an offer."

He gazed intently at her, as if he could read her mind if he looked deeply enough into her eyes.

"Really?" Toni said, fighting back her confusion and fear. "That's fantastic!"

Donovan leaned over and gently kissed her. "I know! Isn't it wonderful? I'm really excited about this position, Toni. You know it's my dream job!" he said, clearing his throat. "So, I accepted the job."

Toni's heart sank. She heard her heart beating in her ears. She suddenly felt sick to her stomach. "Oh," was all she could say. "Um, I'm so happy for you!" she said, trying to sound happy.

He gently stroked her hair, trying to cheer her up. "Look on the bright side, honey. Now you have some place to visit on the West Coast!" he said.

Toni buried her face in her hands and tried not to start crying. Tears streamed down her face anyway. Donovan rubbed her back.

"Don't cry, babe! It's not the end of the world. People have long-distance relationships all the time. You might say it's a fact of life in this new century. People go where the jobs are, and love follows. We can do this," he said. "You'll see."

She stopped hunching over, her eyes to the floor, and she sat up straight and looked him right in the eye. She said, "I don't do long-distance relationships, Donovan. If you really knew me, you'd know that. By taking the job, you're effectively ending our relationship."

"I'm doing no such thing!" he said. He took both her hands in his and squeezed them gently as he leaned forward, practically touching noses with her. "You have to believe me. I want to be with you, but I need to look out for my career too. This kind of opportunity doesn't come along every day. It'll mean a giant pay bump, a benefits package that'd blow your mind, and a retirement plan that could make a big difference for me down the road."

Toni sighed. What he said made sense. Indeed, she'd nagged him to push for bigger clients. Now she wished she'd kept her big mouth shut. She looked away, squeezing her eyes shut in defiance, but he turned her head toward him. "Talk to me, honey. Tell me what's on your mind."

"What do you want me to say?" she asked. "That I want you to go? That everything'll be just peachy? It won't be peachy. And I don't want you to go! I may sound selfish, but after all we've shared for the past six months, I really thought you and I were going somewhere with this relationship."

She paused for a moment, biting her bottom lip, and said, "I … I was falling in love with you."

Donovan cupped her face in his hands. "Toni, the first time I saw you, my heart skipped a beat, I went weak in the knees, and my stomach got tight. I felt in that moment you were the right one for me. And, all the time we've been together, I've never experienced more joy in every way possible. The thought of destroying my relationship with you is heartbreaking. I have to admit this is uncharted territory, and I'm scared to face the unknown. But I have spent my entire life trying to be the best person I could be. To finally have a chance to really go after a great career …" He pulled her close to him. "You understand I would be crazy not to take this position, right?"

Toni did not answer right away. She felt her world was spiraling out of control. As she thought of him being thousands of miles away in California, she wanted to scream. She wanted to beat his chest with both fists. She took a deep breath and said, "I guess I don't have anything else to say right now, other than I wish you all the best!"

She saw him physically flinch. He leaned back on the sofa and stared straight ahead. "Wow, that was pretty cold of you," he said.

"It was meant to be. Look, there's plenty time to talk about this," she said, rising to her feet. "In the meantime, we're going to celebrate this new position. I really am happy for you, Donovan. I just wasn't ready for it. I still have to get my head around the fact you'll be moving all the way across the country."

Donovan stood up. "We can work this out," he said. "You'll see."

She said nothing. Instead, she took his hand and guided him back into her bedroom, where they melted into each other arms with the passion and familiarity of a couple that had been together for years.

20

Lorna stared up at the ceiling of her bedroom, her mind dull and numb. She gingerly felt the bruises on her neck, a frightening reminder of Charles's deadly grip. After spending countless hours contemplating the adverse impact he had on her, she started to hyperventilate. All she could do was close her eyes and allow the tears to stream down her face as she took quick deep breaths to control her panic attack.

For the past few days, she'd taken the time to recuperate at home on bed rest after Charles attacked her. As she lay in bed, she vowed to never again lose herself in a relationship. Her mission was simple. She was going to be strong by any means necessary. She decided it was time to quit licking her wounds and go back to work. She flung back the bed covers, got up, and went into the bathroom to take a shower.

Emerging from the shower, Lorna toweled off, wrapped the towel around her waist, and dried her hair with a blow dryer. Then she selected a red tailored suit and white blouse from the closet, pairing them with neutral stockings and black patent-leather shoes. She tied a red-and-white printed scarf around her neck. She put on her makeup, grabbed her Chanel bag, and headed to the parking garage.

Lorna was in no particular hurry to get to her office, so she decided to drive around to clear her head and to prepare herself psychologically and emotionally to get back to a normal routine. As she drove along the busy streets in the downtown business district with her window open, she listened to the city sounds—car horns honking, street vendors shouting, and air brakes hissing as buses stopped to pick up passengers. People strolled or hurried to their jobs. Others ate breakfast at the sidewalk cafes, walked their dogs, or jogged on this beautiful August day. Thankfully, the typical Atlanta humidity was blissfully absent. She didn't even need the air-conditioner on in the car, which is why she had her window down.

When she pulled into her reserved parking spot, she turned off the engine and looked carefully around her for any signs of Charles. She chided herself for being so paranoid, but she did have good reason to be cautious. He'd been arraigned and released on bail, so he could get her if he was stupid enough to violate a restraining order a second time. Taking a deep breath to calm herself, Lorna opened her car door and climbed out, grabbing her bag from the back seat. Walking toward the entrance, her body stiffened momentarily when she heard footsteps approaching from behind. She whirled around in fear, the temporary serenity she experienced on her drive to work vanishing in a flash of paranoia. No Charles. Just a man about ten feet away. He tipped his hat and nodded.

Once inside the building, Lorna passed the security team at the reception desk, and gave them a forced smile. She was disappointed Scotty wasn't there. She really wanted to thank him again for helping her on that frightful day. She made a mental note to send him a bottle of the single-malt scotch she knew he liked.

She strode through the lobby to the elevator, and moved aside and tightened her grip on her handbag when the door opened and she saw two men inside the car. One was tall, about the same height as Charles, except he was dark-skinned with a shaven head and a bushy moustache. The other was of medium height with an olive complexion, short dark hair, and freckles. She recognized them. They were among the six attorneys who were housed on the floor right above theirs. Toni and one of the senior lawyers had met at a minority economic development board luncheon, and they had intermingled as a group at other functions.

They both stepped aside and smiled brightly, holding the door for her as they said good morning. Lorna forced another smile and entered the car. When she reached her office, she noticed Betty and Alicia huddled at the reception desk sorting the mail. Both smiled broadly at her.

"Good morning, Lorna!" Alicia said. "You must be feeling much better to be back so soon."

"I couldn't stay home brooding," Lorna said. "Not for another minute. Work will keep me focused. Or, so I hope."

Betty said, "That's the spirit! Can't keep a good girl down."

Lorna exchanged some more small talk with them, and then walked the short distance to her suite. She sat down behind her desk, fighting the first signs of another panic attack.

Keep it together, girl! she thought, gripping the arms of her chair. *Don't lose your cool!*

She began to wonder if she'd returned to work too quickly after the assault. Her therapist cautioned her to return to work only when she felt totally ready. She'd been seeing the same shrink off and on for months, but she signed up for weekly sessions after the attack, hoping it would help her resolve the many issues she faced in her personal life.

Charles had really hurt her this time, and he'd also really frightened her. Statistics indicated men like Charles often became obsessed with their victims, sometimes even murdering them, and that seemed to be the case with Charles, at least as far as the obsession part was concerned. She didn't want to give him a second chance to hurt her again.

She took a deep breath and tried to focus on the positives. The panic attack subsided, and the first pangs of an oncoming migraine caused her to squeeze her nose between her right thumb and index finger. She began to massage her temples. Tears welled up in her eyes. She was crying in response to the physical pain, but her tears also came from a place deep within her, a place thick with scar tissue, lost dreams, and failed relationships. Just then, there was a knock on the door. Startled, she sat upright in the chair and wiped away the tears with a tissue.

"Hey, Lorna! Good to see you back," Toni said, taking a seat in one of the chairs facing Lorna's desk. "You okay? You don't look so good."

"Yeah, I'm fine," Lorna said, leaning back in her chair. "I'm still a little spooked by what happened, though. I keep thinking I'll see Charles pop out of nowhere like some sort of screwed up boogeyman."

Toni leaned toward Lorna's desk and said, "You can take more time off, if you think you'll need it."

"I'll get over it. I think being at work will help," Lorna said.

Toni stood up. "Okay, then," she said. She stopped at the office door. "I'm here for you if you ever want to talk. We all are. You know that, don't you?"

"Yeah, I know. Thanks."

"You got it," Toni said, and left Lorna's office.

Lorna reviewed her notes for the meeting with a potential new client. She found it difficult to concentrate, but she figured it was just because she'd been out of the loop for a few days. Yet she continued to feel paranoid. She knew it was irrational to think Charles was hiding around every corner, and was biding his time before launching another assault. She also knew it was tough to control an emotion like fear. It gnawed and nibbled at her constantly, and she worried her current state of mind might reflect a new state of miserable normal. It was especially hard for her to go into the conference room, where the assault occurred. She hesitated at the doorway.

"Get back in the saddle," she whispered. "Come on, girl! You can do this!"

She fought back her anxiety and took a seat at the conference table. She was the first one there. She opened the file containing the proposed marketing services Lorna thought could benefit the potential client, and began going over her notes. She suddenly saw Charles's face inches from hers in a flashback of the beating. She felt the intense pain of his hands pressing on her throat, cutting off her air and causing her to writhe in terror. She forced herself to focus. The time of her appointment with the potential client came and went. Lorna stood up and began pacing. Betty arrived a few minutes later to tell her that the prospect had finally arrived.

Lorna stood up, all smiles and all business. She strode to the door of the conference room to shake hands with Tina Masters, a full-figured woman around forty years old. She wore a wig that sported long blonde hair that hung straight down to just below her shoulders. Her skin was the color of dark chocolate. Tina served as the CEO, marketing director of Applied Learning Technologies, an online education company. Tina had just landed a nice chunk of change from a bunch of venture capitalists, and she was looking to hire a PR agency to ramp up the marketing and public relations campaigns needed to launch the company in just the right way.

"Ms. Masters," Lorna said, "so nice to meet you after all this time on the phone and via email."

Tina shook Lorna's hand and apologized for being late.

"Traffic in the loop was a real bear this morning. I finally had to get off and take the back way."

"Come ... have a seat." Lorna gestured toward the conference table.

Both ladies sat down. Just then, Lorna's cell phone chimed. She looked down at the screen and felt a wave of fear. The message was from Charles. *When will this asshole ever learn?*

She pressed delete. For the longest time, she'd convinced herself Charles would change, that he was capable of true love, and his problems could be solved with therapy. She'd also believed him when he said he was sorry and he'd never hit her again. Well, now, she didn't believe him anymore. Not one stinking bit. Charles could go rot in hell as far as she was concerned.

21

It had been a tough three days since Audrey broke off her relationship with David. She had not slept much, and to keep from going insane she kept busy by cleaning and re-cleaning her closet. Her stomach felt nauseous, leaving her without much of an appetite. Half eaten plates of food were left on the coffee table in the living room. She only managed to eat bowls of soup and crackers, and drank plenty of water simply to survive.

Although, on a rational level, she knew everyone struggled in their professional and personal lives, she wondered why she felt so broken. She'd felt this way all her life in one way or another. She'd led a relatively good childhood. Her parents were decent, hardworking people who had loved her with all their hearts. Yet she always seemed to pick the worst possible men as potential dates, and these men reinforced her emotional insecurities. Indeed, these men preyed on them. Not all of them were as bad as Lorna's friend, Charles, but some were.

David's failure to reveal the role his supposed ex-girlfriend would play in his life indicated she couldn't trust him. The only reason she knew about Sheila in the first place was because she caught him with her when she unexpectedly came to see him at his apartment. While he'd sworn, he'd be faithful to her, Audrey believed the situation represented nothing more than a ticking timebomb that would ultimately blow their relationship sky high, and she felt he would eventually sleep with Sheila. It was inevitable, especially after the baby was born and she got her figure back. And she was having David's baby, which meant that the child would forever be in his life, as would she, his ex-girlfriend. It had taken a lot of courage for her to break up with David, but she realized it was best to tear the Band-Aid off sooner rather than later.

The breakup hit her hard, though. Finding it difficult to be around anyone else, she told Toni she would be working from home for a couple days. Toni and Lorna asked what was wrong, but Audrey didn't feel like going into details at the moment. She still didn't.

The phone rang in her home office. She ignored the incoming call, although she knew she should probably pick up. She simply didn't want to talk with anyone. It just seemed easier to avoid people for the time being. She concentrated on the document she was working on.

Later that afternoon, the doorbell rang. Assuming it was probably David, she didn't budge from her home office. She had ignored the ringing of her home and cell phone when he'd called in the past few days, and allowed his pleas for a reconciliation to go to voicemail. Suddenly, there was a banging on her door.

"Audrey, I know you're in there. Come on! Open up!" Toni shouted, banging on the door again, only more insistently this time.

Knowing that Toni was not about to quit bothering her, she stalked to the front door and opened it.

"Jeez," Toni said. "You look like death warmed over. Can I come in?"

Audrey nodded toward the living room. "Sure. Since you're here."

She followed Toni into the living and sat down across from her in the loveseat. "So, what's up?"

"We've been trying to reach you all morning to include you in an important conference call," Toni said. "Really, this whole thing is ridiculous. First it was Lorna with her personal issues declaring she'd work from home, and now you. How in the hell are we expected to run a business like this? I know you're heartbroken over David's lies and betrayals, but you really did the right thing in ditching his sorry ass. You know that, don't you?"

Audrey crossed her right leg over her left. She sighed and said, "In my head I know I did the right thing. My heart disagrees."

"That's pretty obvious. You know, I don't mean to be cavalier an all, but this too shall pass. Just give it time," Toni said.

"I guess you think I'm pretty messed up."

Toni got up from the couch, walked over Audrey, who was still sitting on the loveseat, knelt, and hugged her. "Maybe I would have agreed with you in the past. But, lately, after all we've been through, you're no more screwed up than the rest of us."

"I guess you're right about that."

"I have an idea," Toni said. "Come on, get dressed. We're going out to happy hour!"

Audrey knew resistance was futile. She didn't even bother to argue. Instead, she resigned herself to being forced outside of her insular shell at home into the bustle of the world outside.

Hell, she thought, *maybe it'll do me good to get out of here for a while.*

When Audrey finished getting ready, she and Toni rode the elevator down to the parking garage, hopped in Toni's Porsche, and they hit their favorite bar and grill trying to help Audrey forget all about her troubles with David.

"Okay, sweetie," Toni said, "you're spent."

Audrey burped, finishing off her margarita. "I don't feel so good."

"Let's get you home to bed," Toni said, her voice gentle and full of empathy.

The drive home was nothing but a blur. Audrey's head spun. She wasn't much of a drinker, so the numerous margaritas went straight to her head. Toni pulled up in front of the building.

"You sure you don't want me to walk you up?" Toni asked.

Audrey said she was sure. She grinned stupidly as she got out of the car. "See you soon," she said, and weaved up to the door. The doorman wished her a good evening as he let her in. She took the elevator up to her apartment, and fumbled with the keys. For some strange reason, the lock kept moving around. She kept trying to insert the key, and finally hit paydirt on the fourth try. Audrey staggered into bed and passed out.

When she woke up, her dress was lying on the floor, and she was still wearing her stockings, panties, and bra. She had a queasy stomach, headache, and a sore throat. All a clear sign she'd partied way too much with Toni the night before. Audrey slowly got up from the bed, running her fingers through her tangled hair. She put on her robe as she made her way to the kitchen to turn on the coffeemaker.

Minutes later, the coffee finished brewing. She poured a cup and slumped into the chair at the kitchen table, her eyes closing in contentment as she leaned back, one leg tucked under her, and her warm mug in her right hand. She still felt sad about David, and she knew it would be a long time before she would ever trust another man, let alone allow him into her heart and her bed. Taking another sip of coffee, she thought back on the previous night of craziness with her best friend.

At Toni's insistence, the two of them spent happy hour at the new bar and grill on Peachtree Street. It was spacious with hardwood floors. A smoking section occupied the back area, a long bar occupied the middle of the establishment, and there were separate rooms for games, dancing, and karaoke. It had been Mexican night, so after settling in at a cozy booth, they dove into the complimentary bowl of chips and salsa. For dinner, they ordered chicken and beef quesadillas, and a pitcher of margaritas.

Toni poured their drinks. She held hers up and said, "Cheers! Here's to good friends."

"I'll drink to that," Audrey said, trying to sound cheerful. She knew she was failing miserably at putting a brave face on how she felt. She stifled a sob. Toni noticed, reaching across the table and patting her left hand.

"Now, now. We aren't supposed to feel sad on a night like this. You're here to get your mind off your troubles, not to dwell on them."

"I'm sorry, Toni, but I have to talk about it."

"I'm all ears."

"I wonder all the time about when I'm going to meet an upwardly mobile man who's interested in getting to know me from the neck up. You saw how I handled things back in the day. I've made a lot of bad choices in my life, but this time I feel so freaking embarrassed by yet another failed relationship. What's wrong with me?"

Toni held out her hand across the table. Audrey hesitated before taking it into hers.

"Oh, Red, I understand how you might be feeling. There is absolutely nothing wrong with you. You're a beautiful, free-spirited, kind-hearted woman. The only thing wrong is you're going through a tough time, that's all. But hard times are sometimes a blessing in disguise."

"What exactly does that mean?" Audrey asked.

"I think we tend to focus on the negativity instead of the positive. You know I'm a true believer in the concept of self-talk. We can actually talk ourselves into a funk, if we let the negative thoughts run wild. Even worse, if we encourage them. One negative thought will give birth to another, and another."

"Yeah, yeah, yeah, I get it, Toni. But I think bad is usually just bad. It's not a blessing in disguise. It's not an opportunity. It's just bad."

"Nothing in this world is black and white," Toni said. "The world is a mix of darkness and light … usually resulting in gray. You can look at your relationship with David as a learning experience."

"Yeah, the only thing this has taught me is I suck at choosing men."

"No. It taught you that you have the inner strength to change course if you don't think you're on the right track. To me, that represents a major step forward for you," Toni said.

And the conversation had continued, until they decided to try their hand at karaoke. Their performance drew the attention of two good looking guys in their early thirties. Steve and Barry, as she recalled. Barry had obviously been smitten with her, which helped build her confidence, even if she had no intention of getting back into a relationship any time soon. Interestingly enough, the guys were thinking of starting their own IT company, and they could turn out to be potential future clients. If that panned out, then the evening wasn't a total waste.

She took another sip of coffee, and then got up from the kitchen table to make some toast. She thought about her life as she cut up a grapefruit. She sensed a change was coming. She just didn't know what it would be.

22

Toni sat at her computer drafting yet another proposal for expanding the company. She hit a wall about halfway through the project. Sighing, she stood up, stretched, and walked over to the window. Her shoulders slumped as she looked out at the spectacular view. In many ways, the view, the very office itself, stood as byproducts of her stellar success in business. She'd literally climbed her way up the ivory towers in marketing and advertising to arrive at an immensely comfortable perch. Yet she still didn't feel complete, whole, content, or even happy most of the time. She'd tried online dating to fill a hole inside her, and, instead, she'd dug the hole deeper.

Toni began pacing, the proposal temporarily forgotten. She clasped her hands behind her back. It occurred to her the one constant in life was change. Change occurred in business all the time, and if a person was really living life instead of going through it by rote, change occurred in one's personal life on a regular basis as well. She thought about Donovan. A golden opportunity just fell out of the clear blue sky right into his lap.

You could go with him, she told herself. *You could follow him to Silicon Valley.*

She dismissed the thought as impossible. No way was she giving up all she'd worked on to follow a man all the way across the country. He'd brought the option up, and she'd immediately squashed the idea. But the seed had been planted. She just didn't want to water it at the moment, but, she conceded, she might change her mind. Time was running out, though. Donovan was due to leave for his new job in a matter of days. She stopped pacing and returned to the window, her mood deeply contemplative, something of a rarity for her.

It was late afternoon transitioning into evening. Busy people made their way in the streets below trying to make it home from work. Toni's attention focused on a young couple standing in front of the building across the way. She presumed the man was picking up his wife from work. He took her into his arms, squeezing her to his chest. They stayed that way for a moment with his chin on her head. Finally, she lifted her head to look at him and they kissed. Then he escorted her over to a black Mercedes Benz sedan, holding the door for her as she glided into the seat.

Hmmm, they seem so in love. Probably recently married and still in their honeymoon phase.

Toni could not help but feel a bitter taste in her mouth. Crossing her arms over her chest, she muttered, "Love. Who needs it?"

Biting her bottom lip, she sat down at her desk to return a few phone calls. She'd deal with the rest of the proposal later. The intercom buzzed. Toni pressed to answer.

"Yes, Betty."

"Donovan is on the line. Should I transfer him?"

Toni checked the clock on her desk. It was 6:45 p.m.

"Yeah, put him through."

"Will do. I'm leaving now. See ya tomorrow," she said.

"Thanks, Betty. Get home safe," she said, and hit the button for the line Donovan was holding on.

Donovan had called her earlier and said he'd made reservations at a swanky rooftop restaurant at the Hyatt Regency Hotel on Peachtree Street. He told her that he'd spent the day with the movers packing up his belongings to get them transported to California ahead of him. The company was paying for the move, and the movers would unpack after offloading the stuff into the nice little condo Donovan had rented. She made arrangements to pick him up at his office. A short time later, he was seated beside her in the car.

On the drive to the restaurant, Toni noticed Donovan didn't talk much. She understood why. The evening was supposed to be a pleasant goodbye, but the imminent separation weighed on her. She could tell it weighed on Donovan as well.

"I'm going to miss you terribly," Donovan said.

She glanced at him for a second before turning her eyes back on the road. "Back at you," she said. "Just when things were getting serious too. It really sucks you have to go."

"I can't pass on this job, Toni. You know that."

Exhaling loudly and shaking her head in frustration at the apparent permanent impasse, she said, "And I can't give up my PR agency. Not after working so hard to make it a success during these past five years. You know it's not fair to ask me to give up my dream for yours. This is a brand-new century, Donovan. Things don't work the way they once did."

She eased around a delivery truck. "Ah, there it is," she said, nodding toward the hotel. "Hey, let's make a promise to each other tonight. Let's keep it light. Nothing heavy."

"Done and done!" Donovan said, shooting her a warm smile.

Although it was dark in the car, she knew his deep brown eyes had twinkled when he'd said that.

They pulled up in front of the hotel, and the valet took care of parking the Porsche. Toni hadn't been to the hotel before, and it indeed struck her as grand. When she stepped into the restaurant on the twenty-second floor, she almost gasped at the stunning nature of the 360-degree view. The bright lights of the city spread out at her feet, and, just for a moment, she felt like the world possessed limitless possibilities. She took Donovan by the right hand and squeezed as she watched the view change as the entire restaurant slowly rotated.

"This is awesome," she said.

"Absolutely," he said.

They were soon seated at a nice cozy table by the window. "I've always wanted to come here, but I could never seem to find the time," Toni said. "Like I said. The view is awe inspiring. Thanks so much for choosing such a romantic place for our last dinner together."

"You mean our last dinner together in Atlanta for the moment. I assume we'll both be racking up the frequent flyer miles in the coming months."

Toni nodded. "You may be right about that."

Toni felt a surge of affection for Donovan. He looked so handsome. She suddenly had an irresistible urge to lean over and kiss him, but they were interrupted by the waiter who offered them a basket of warm, fresh rolls in one hand, and the menus and wine list in the other.

They ordered their meals and savored a crisp merlot. Toni sometimes veered into the heavy, and Donovan always nudged the conversation back to the light side. She appreciated it. His sensitivity appealed to her. When she talked, he really seemed to listen. He was different in so many ways, and that was one of them. The other night when she took Audrey out to cheer her up, Audrey complained about how hard it was to find an upwardly mobile man with a bright future and the good sense to love her for who she was, not what she looked like. She realized she had found exactly that in Donovan, and she felt sad the relationship was about to dramatically change whether either of them wanted it to or not.

Throughout the remainder of the evening as they settled into their meals and listened to the background jazz music, Toni experienced a rollercoaster of emotions. She kept them tamped down as best as she could. She noticed he was staring at her intently. There was something sexy in his eyes. Or, maybe it was the two glasses of wine she drank. She sensed he wanted to say something, but she didn't know what.

"So, tell me, Donovan, what's on your mind? I know we said we wouldn't get heavy, and I think we've done a terrific job at it so far. But I'm feeling conflicted, a little mixed up, and I think you are too."

Donovan cleared his throat. "That's true. I am. And I'm not sure what to do about it. Everything seems to be out of our control. You have to stay in Atlanta, and I have to move to California. Why do great things always seem to require some kind of sacrifice? It just doesn't seem fair to me."

Toni laughed ruefully. "No, it doesn't. So, spit it out, Donovan. Penny for your thoughts."

Donovan took her hands in both of his. She saw true sadness in his eyes, and it broke her heart.

"I know we've already talked about how to keep our relationship going long distance, but I can't help but wonder how our relationship might have evolved if I wasn't moving to California."

"Great minds think alike," Toni said. "I've been hung up on the same thing. I guess it's a matter of entertaining the what-ifs as opposed to the what is. The wondering what would've happened if I'd done this or that. The looking back over your shoulder. All that second guessing."

"I guess it is what it is," Donovan said. He killed the rest of the wine in his glass, picked up the empty bottle, and frowned. "You want another one?"

Toni shook her head no. "I don't want to dull my sensations for the evening, if you catch my drift."

Donovan laughed. "Oh, I got your drift, honey. Big time. I'm really gonna miss your drift too!"

Now it was Toni's turn to laugh. Then she got serious again. "When I first met you, I wasn't ready for love, but because we connected so fast, well, frankly, it scared the hell out of me, which is one reason why it took so long for us to finally meet in person. I procrastinated because I didn't want to get hurt."

Donovan gently clasped the fingers of her right hand in his, and kissed the manicured tips one by one, sending crazy hot energy pulsing through her.

"Baby, I'm so sorry. You're one special lady, and I feel lucky to have met you. I wish I didn't have to hurt you like this. I'm hurting too, you know."

"I know," Toni said, withdrawing her hand from his.

"I'm so looking forward to spending the rest of the weekend with you. Because honestly, I want to take you back to your place right now and make passionate love to you all night long. Long and slow. Real slow, my sweet sunshine."

Toni swallowed hard. "I hoped that was on the itinerary," she said.

Donovan grinned from ear-to-ear as he summoned the waiter for the check. He paid up, and they drove back to Toni's condo for what she hoped would be a mighty sexy sendoff.

At least he'll be on the plane worn out and with a big ol' smile on his face, she thought playfully, warming to what she knew would be a hot lovemaking session. On the way, they chatted amiably. Whenever Donovan glanced at her, he reached over to touch her face, and Toni playfully swatted his hand away. They parked and took the elevator up to her condo. She was aware of the sexual tension in the air. She could practically cut it with a knife. Once inside, Toni dropped her purse and keys on the credenza, and kicked off her heels. While Donovan sauntered over to the couch and collapsed, she went to the liquor cabinet.

"Would you like a glass of cabernet sauvignon?" she asked.

"That sounds great!"

She poured two glasses of wine, returned to the couch, placed the drinks on the coffee table, and sat beside him. After a moment, Donovan reached over and glided his finger alongside her cheekbone. Toni nervously turned her head to him and smiled.

"Have I told you how adorable you are?" he asked.

She laughed. "Only about three times tonight. But who's counting?"

"Well, come over here, and let me show you what I mean."

He wrapped an arm around her waist, pulling her close to him. Toni responded by shifting her body and tilting her head back.

"I can't get you off my mind," he said, before pressing his face against her neck and kissing her there.

Toni ran her fingers through his hair.

"There is nothing I wouldn't do for you. Absolutely nothing," he said, breathing hard against her moist lips, exploring her mouth with his tongue. The wine on the coffee table remained untouched as his hand started wandering up her dress.

Then they paused kissing for a moment, and Toni said, "I think it's time to prove it."

Donovan's eyes were wide and filled with enthusiasm. He gave her a wolfish grin. "Lead the way, baby."

Toni rose to her feet and took Donovan's hand. As he eagerly slipped out of his shoes, she led him into her bedroom. Donovan was on her in an instant. She pushed him playfully away.

"Easy does it now. Let's make this night one to remember, shall we?" she asked. She stepped close, looked up into his eyes, and placed her right index finger over his lips. "Now you hush and let your lady take care of things from here on out, okay?"

Donovan looked at her as if he hadn't eaten in years. The hunger in him was plain, and it really turned her on. She pranced over to the dresser on the far side of the room and took two scented candles from the top drawer.

"Lavender," she said. "it's supposed to be calming. Peaceful. It's one of my favorite colors, you know."

"How could I not know?" he said.

She lit the candles, and luxuriated in the subtle fragrance that almost immediately filled the bedroom. She turned the lights off, and faced him. "I want to make this an unforgettable night," she said.

"Let's make it happen," he said.

Donovan wrapped his arms around her waist and kissed her neck. She leaned against his broad shoulders, accepting his love with abandon. His hands moved down to her hips, and he began to slowly move her toward the bed until they were standing beside it. Her heart fluttered as he unzipped her dress. She lowered her arms from around his neck and allowed the dress to fall to the floor.

Toni pulled away from him and quickly unbuttoned his shirt, dropping it on the floor next to her dress. Then she reached down to unbuckle his belt. In one fell swoop, his pants dropped to the floor. Toni traced her hands over his bare chest as he gently guided her back and they tumbled onto the king-size bed. As he lay down beside her on his side, he held her head while kissing her passionately. Toni arched her back and Donovan unclasped her bra with ease. Reaching down, he ran his fingertips along the edge of her silky panties.

"I think these things need to go too," he said, tossing her panties to the side of the bed.

He blazed a trail of hot kisses on her bare shoulders, up the nape of her neck, and then he playfully nibbled at her earlobe while he slipped out of his boxer shorts.

She closed her eyes and whispered, "Oh, Don-o-van."

"I'm right here, baby," Donovan said.

Toni grasped the back of his neck, rising up to meet him as he glided inside her. The passion between them exploded in a frenzy of bliss. Toni tried to restrain herself, then she tried to restrain him to make it last as long as possible. The first round of lovemaking diminished their immediate hunger, and the second round rocketed into the realm of the gift of a love that remained undiscovered in life, unless you got really lucky. The trick with true love was you had to keep your eyes open, or it could sneak right on by without your even knowing you had a shot at finding it.

Although Toni wasn't thinking such things during their lovemaking, the realization spotting true love actually took a conscious effort slowly began to dawn on her as she snuggled against Donovan while he snored. As she lay in bed staring up at the ceiling in the dimness of her bedroom, she wondered if she hadn't been blind to true love during her meteoric rise to riches and power in the business world.

Did the love of money blind me to what really matters? she wondered. *Could I really be that shallow?*

She considered her life, her perspective on it, and the way she dealt with people on all levels. She admitted she liked to be in the driver's seat, and she didn't like it when her colleagues questioned her decisions. She admitted she behaved similarly in her personal life. When it came to sex, she wanted to be the mover and the shaker, the supreme decision-maker.

You hush now, girl, she told herself. *You best get some sleep, or you'll never be able to get up in the morning.*

She tried to shut her mind off, but it wasn't easy. She kept reliving her lovemaking session with Donovan again and again, until she finally drifted off to sleep. When she woke up with a start, it seemed to her she'd just dozed off for a few seconds, but a glance at the alarm clock on the nightstand told it was seven o-clock. She'd drank and made love so hard the previous evening, and now she was paying for it. The cold hard reality that Donovan was leaving for California hit home once again.

"Oh, God," she whispered, her shoulders shaking as she quietly cried, hoping she wouldn't wake Donovan up. She felt alone with nothing but her thoughts and fears to envelop her. She gently pulled back the covers and got up. Putting on her satin bathrobe, she walked across her bedroom to the bathroom. She pulled her hair back before turning on the shower. She stepped into the shower and let the hot water run over her as she thought about what was left of the weekend. She had already filled up the cabinets and fridge with provisions. As it was expected they were going to spend time at her place, there would be enough food to last them for the next two days. When she finished showering, she dried off and put on her underwear. She was heading for her walk-in closet when she saw Donovan sitting up in bed, partially covered with the bedsheets from his waist down.

He was looking at her. "Morning sunshine," he said, his voice deep and warm.

She hesitated, stopping in midstride. "Oh, I didn't know you were up," she said. "I hope I didn't wake you. I tried to be quiet."

"Oh, I'm up all right," he said.

Toni smiled at the suggestive tone of his voice.

"Are you now?" she said. "Just how up is up?"

"Pretty far up the flagpole, I'd say." Donovan patted the bed. "Come here, sexy. Lemme show you just how far up the flagpole I can go!"

Toni did a fake fashion runway walk from the closet to the bed, sashaying with exaggerated swings of her hips. "You like?" she asked, stopping at the edge of the bed.

"I like very, very much," Donovan said.

She leaned over and kissed him tenderly. "I like you very much too."

She sat down on the bed next to him. "Let's do it again," she whispered.

Donovan needed no convincing. This time when they finished making morning love, Toni got up, took another shower, and got dressed. She went into the kitchen to make breakfast while Donovan showered. She simultaneously felt good and bad. For one thing, she relished the time she was spending with Donovan, but the fact that the time they had left together was certainly finite detracted from the specialness of it. Indeed, she realized his leaving had triggered some deep-seated psychological issues she had buried since she was a little girl.

Donovan came out just then. She smiled wanly when she saw him. She said, "Hey." Then she went back to mixing the pancake batter.

"Hay is for horses," Donovan said with a laugh, and then he made a really silly attempt to sound like a horse.

"You're an idiot, you know that?" she said. "Coffee's ready. Pour yourself a mug."

"Don't mind if I do," he said. Donovan made himself some coffee and sat down at the kitchen table while Toni dished some cantaloupe into two bowls.

"Is there something you want to talk about?" Donovan asked.

"What'd you mean?" she asked with feigned nonchalance as she continued making breakfast with her back to him. "Talk about what?"

"You just seem a little off."

"Of course, I'm a little off! You're leaving me to take a job all the way across the entire God damned country!" she yelled, throwing the stirring spoon into the sink with such force it flew out and fell on the floor, depositing spatters of batter as it went. "Shit. Now look what you made me do," she said, grabbing a sponge and dabbing up the batter.

"Hey, hey! Chill out! I didn't mean anything by what I said. I just said you seem a bit off this morning."

"Now who's got hay for horses," she said.

Toni rinsed the stirring spoon off and vigorously beat the batter again. She realized she needed to connect the dots for Donovan. These were dots that had just become clear to her in a flash of understanding when it came to her own inner world of emotions.

"I think one of the reasons why I'm taking your move so hard is it brings back the feelings of abandonment I experienced when I was a kid in foster care. I've told you all about that."

"Yeah, it sounded really rough."

"It was. I think the insecurity I felt as a kid is part of why I come off so assertive as an adult. I think it's also part of why I shy away from relationships with men. The relationships always end for one reason or another, and I'm always left alone holding the damned bag. Frankly, I'm getting sick of it, Donovan. So, while I'm trying to put a brave face on your leaving, I'm having a hard time with it, as you well know."

Donovan got up from the table and hugged her. He gently kissed her on the lips. She didn't put her arms around him. He stepped back. "You know I love you, right?" he asked.

"Then don't go!" she said, realizing she sounded like she was whining.

"Let's not go there. Let's not ruin what started as a fantastic morning. Let's not ruin what time we have left together."

She knew he was right. They'd talked and argued, and then they'd kissed and made up on so many occasions that the conversation was starting to sound like a broken record.

Just leave it alone, okay? she chided herself.

"Okay, let's put a lid on it," Toni said. "I promise to try anyway. I don't want to ruin any of our last minutes together."

"Deal," Donovan said. "Now let me help you fix breakfast."

23

Toni slowed her Porsche down just a bit to let a semi pass her on the left. The big rig shook the little sports car as it passed.

"Asshole," Donovan said. He flipped the truck the bird even though the driver was long gone.

"Aren't we in a good mood this morning," Toni said, glancing over at him in the passenger seat.

"You're in a good mood?"

"Ha! Hell no!" Toni said. "I'm in a terrible mood. Just plain terrible."

"Thought so."

"Why would I be in a good mood when I'm driving you to the airport to put you on a plane so you can jet right on out of my life? Probably forever. Why would that ever put me in a good mood?"

Donovan didn't answer what she figured he thought was a rhetorical question. She focused on the road ahead. The smooth melodies of easy jazz helped reduce the tension in the air. She'd told him she thought they should probably just end the relationship. She didn't think trying to maintain a long-distance relationship made much sense. Their love was strong at the moment, but it would fade just like all the rest of the loves she'd known in her life. Granted, there weren't many.

She'd always guarded herself against the cold, cruel world to prevent more damage from being done by virtue of simply being alive. Life was hard enough without inviting more hassles, and more dishonesty than already existed in daily living on multiple levels so pervasive she'd decided ages ago to pull up her proverbial drawbridge to keep the invaders at bay. She was self-aware enough to know that was exactly what she was doing at that very moment.

You know the drill, girl. You know how this will all end up. Why should this time be any different from the last times?

Toni remained largely silent for the rest of the trip to the airport. She parked in the temporary lot, and they entered the airport together. She tried to keep her emotions tamped down, and was having a hard time doing it. She took Donovan's hand in hers as they walked through security to the west gate departure area. She sat down on one of the grimy plastic seats, folded her hands in her lap, and stared out the expansive bank of windows at the airfield.

"This is all a bit much for me to take, you know," she said, her voice barely above a whisper.

Donovan put his right arm around her shoulders and pulled her close. He whispered in her ear. "It's hard for me too. I know this separation isn't going to be easy. I know you wanted to end the relationship and I'm glad I was able to talk you out of such foolishness. We just have to stand tough together, and we'll come out all the stronger on the other end."

He gently touched the bottom of her chin, and moved her head ever so slightly so she could look at him directly. The sadness in Donovan's eyes almost made her break down in tears. She fought back the despair she felt.

"We can only take things one step at a time," he said. "I know you don't want to give up your business to be with me in California. I understand that. I actually admire you for your strength and conviction. But putting a false end on what could be a loving long-term relationship just because a career move means we have to be apart for a while doesn't make any sense."

"But—"

"But nothin'!" Donovan said. He squeezed her shoulder. "You'll see. You'll see I'm right and you have nothin' to worry about in the least. We can make this work, Toni. We really can, if we both try real hard to be sensitive to each other's needs."

"I hope you're right. I don't think you are, and I hope I'm wrong about that."

The boarding call for Donovan's flight stopped the conversation. Sighing, he gently drew her to him. They hugged for a long moment, and then he kissed her softly and with great sensitivity. There was no passion. There was no red-hot fire of unabashed lust. There was only the parting of two lovers, and the uncertain future Toni knew would determine whether she would end up with the guy of her dreams, or with a lump of coal in her Christmas stocking. At the moment, she was pessimistic enough to go with the coal, and not with the happy ending she so desperately wanted. Life just wasn't fair, and she figured the sooner she accepted the unpleasant reality the sooner she could harden up her heart and just keep on going her own way no matter what anyone else thought, said, or did.

"Well, I guess this is me," Donovan said, stating the obvious. He stood up, grabbed his carry-on bag.

Feeling a little dizzy and light headed, Toni got to her feet. She put both arms around his neck and drew him close, resting her head on his chest. The troubles of the world seemed to fade away when she was in his arms. She felt protected, loved, and nurtured. Donovan had never given her pause, never made her feel less than the woman she was, and seldom even made her angry. They were simpatico from the first email they'd exchanged on the Soulfully Yours dating website, and the fact he was leaving her was almost too much for her to bear. Abandonment was a core issue with her. Her fear of it had made her withdraw behind a fortress of assertive go-getter female power that intimidated most men, but not Donovan. He'd told her he liked strong women.

"I like a woman who's not afraid to speak her mind, and who's not afraid of the world at large. I love that about you, Toni. You're the embodiment of lady power, and I think it suits you to a tee. It's one of the things about you that really turns me on."

He'd consistently said other similar things to her, all of which contributed to her burgeoning feelings of love for him.

"I'm going to miss you *this* much," Toni said, holding both arms straight out.

Donovan laughed. "You're crazy!"

"Back at ya!" Toni said.

"I don't like long goodbyes," Donovan said. "Besides, this isn't goodbye. It's simply a see ya soon kinda thing."

Toni swallowed hard. Her throat felt tight. She found it difficult to breathe. "I know, honey," she said.

Donovan kissed her and held her close for another long moment. The boarding announcement broke the moment.

"I have to go," he said.

A lone tear trickled down Toni's cheek. Donovan dabbed it with his right index finger and touched her lips with his moist fingertip.

"I'll call you when I get in," he said, and hurried to the gate.

Toni watched him go, the rending of her heart almost complete. She walked to the window and stared blankly at the plane on the tarmac. She waited until the aircraft taxied away, then she left the airport and drove to work in a dull haze she knew would last as long as it did until she could get on with her busy life without the pesky interference of something that brought nothing but grief and pain—love, and all it stood for. She just didn't want to admit to herself despite her fears and trepidation she had fallen head over heels in love with Donovan, and it would take a conscious effort to get over him.

Get over it, girl! she thought. *Don't be a fool for any man. Not for any man in the whole big wide world.*

When Toni returned home from work that evening, she was physically and emotionally exhausted. She paused in the foyer, keenly aware of the faint scent of Donovan's Brut cologne. She kicked off her shoes, set her purse and keys on the credenza, and went straight to the kitchen for something to eat. Standing in front of the open fridge, she devoured two leftover fried chicken legs and the last of the pasta salad. She felt so hollow it seemed no amount of food could fill her.

She walked into the living room and poured a shot glass of bourbon, drinking the liquor straight with no chaser. It was a strong drink, but she needed it. She sat down on the couch and rested her head on a pillow, not being able to stand the thought of spending the night alone in the bed she had shared with Donovan for the past six months. If only she had him to console her with a kiss and a caress—if just to let her know she would never be lonely again, even though she knew deep down in her heart nobody could ever promise another person that loneliness would forever be banished from life.

The humidity of a typical Georgia summer slowly gave way to the drier and cooler air that sagged south from Canada, starting as early as October. In an attempt to dull the pain, she felt in being apart from Donovan, Toni threw herself into her work with even more fervor than ever before. She knew she was acting like a hamster on a spinning wheel, and she didn't care. The agency was taking off financially, in part because of the fabulous story about the firm that was published in *Atlanta Magazine*. At any rate, Toni wasn't about to look a gift horse in the mouth. She was thrilled that the company was reaping new business by the bushel. The more she had on her plate, the less she had time to brood over her apparently consistent failure in the men's department.

Her two best friends also pushed ahead with their emotional blinders on. Between Lorna and the Charles disaster, and Audrey and David's initial subterfuge with Sheila in the rearview mirror, hopefully the whole shebang was finished for good. For Toni's part, her prediction the long-distance relationship between her and Donovan would probably not work out seemed to be coming true. She'd flown out to San Francisco one time, and he'd flown back east to Georgia, as well. They'd had a great time together, especially in bed, but with each passing month Toni felt the distance grow between them. It was almost as if they needed the physical connection to really cement the deal. It was almost as if the physical was the glue that held them together, and the emotional and intellectual bond was weaker than she cared to admit. The very notion disturbed Toni when she allowed herself to think the sole driver behind her attraction to Donovan was simply physical in nature. If that was the case, then what did that say about her as a person? As a woman?

It seemed like these kinds of thoughts percolated whenever Toni had a spare minute, and that was true as she arrived home from work especially bushed in the evenings. Autumn was always a busy time, and the fall of the year 2000 was no exception. Most of her clients wanted to ramp up marketing and public relations efforts in advance of the holidays, which meant Toni had to work relentlessly to ensure each client received the top-notch service they were entitled to.

Toni took a hot shower, put on her pajamas, and stretched out on top of her bedspread, her back propped up on the pillows stacked against the headboard. She'd missed a call from Donovan earlier in the day, and she decided to see if she could get him on the line now. She glanced at the clock on the nightstand next to the bed. It would be about nine in the evening on the West Coast. There was a chance he'd be home.

She dialed Donovan's number, and when he answered they exchanged greetings, and then some small talk. It felt good to just talk with him. The sound of his voice calmed her, and she wondered about how cruel life could be to send her a wonderful man only to snatch him away through no fault of either party. The irony was not lost on her.

"You know I miss you like crazy," Donovan said.

Toni sighed. "I know. I miss you too. Sometimes I get so lonely here I could cry."

Silence.

"Uh, Toni?" Donovan said, "I had an idea the other day that I wanted to run by you."

Toni sat up straighter in bed. "Oh, yeah? What?"

"Did you ever consider expanding the agency to include an office in San Francisco?"

Toni laughed. "I suppose the thought has crossed my mind. It just doesn't seem practical at this time, though. You know how it is. The agency's going great guns right now, and I don't want to take my eyes off the ball. Opening a new satellite office would only be a major distraction."

More silence.

"You're in the driver's seat, Toni. If you want to, you could put Audrey in charge of the Georgia branch, and you could move out here to open up the new office. Think of all the money you could make."

She heard annoyance in his voice, and she didn't understand why he was getting irritated with her. She also felt her own consternation rising. For a shrewd guy, Donovan could be real sensitive at times, as was the case with most, if not all, men.

"You're not wanting to even consider the option hurts me," Donovan said. "It makes me feel like you don't love me enough to move heaven and earth to be with me. What's up with that?"

Toni squeezed the receiver tight. Barely fighting back the urge to shout at him, she said, "You've got some God damned nerve. You're the one who moved to California, not me. This is all on you. Don't put this on me. No friggin' way!"

Silence.

"You hear me, Donovan? Don't put any of this shit on me. No way. No how."

"I hear you," he said, sounding defeated. "I'm sorry. I didn't mean to piss you off."

"Well, you did. Look, I gotta go. I got a killer day tomorrow."

The end of the conversation was awkward and strained, and she was relieved when the call ended. She certainly did think of expanding the business to the West Coast, and she thought such a major move might happen at some point in the future whether she was with Donovan or not. She was wary about rushing into something so drastic solely on the count of wanting to be near a man. She asked herself what would happen if she fell out of love with him. Would she have opened the West Coast office without Donovan in the picture? Yet the notion of opening a new office in San Francisco did not vanish entirely. It remained firmly rooted in the back of her mind as a possible option to pursue.

Yawning, Toni leaned over and switched off the lamp on the nightstand next to the bed. She sprawled out on her back with her eyes wide open as she contemplated where she was at in life, and the tears came and did not stop until she finally drifted off into a fitful sleep.

Toni arrived at the agency with little time to spare before the ten o'clock team meeting. She checked in with Betty at the front desk, retrieved the messages from the evening before, and walked down the hallway to her office. As she passed Alicia's office, the newly promoted Communications Coordinator hurried out from behind her desk.

"Morning, Toni!" Alicia said, meeting Toni at the door.

Toni wished Alicia a good morning as well.

"I can't believe all this new business we've been getting as a result of that story in *Atlanta Magazine*," Alicia said. "It's really phenomenal."

Toni laughed. Smiling broadly at Alicia, she said, "And how! We could only dream we'd get results like this. Incredible, really. But I should say I'm not totally surprised. I mean, look at the dream team we put together. Solid gold. Top flight. What's not to love?"

"You got that right," Alicia said. She leaned against the door with her hip, ran her hand through her hair, and shook her head. "I guess it's a make hay while the sun shines sort of thing. There are so many calls coming in from all these companies, I couldn't sleep last night. I must have woken up a hundred times. So, I decided to come in early to catch up on some paperwork."

Toni smiled and put a hand on her shoulder. "Well, I must say I love your attitude. It's great to see you're enthused with your new assignment."

"Thanks, Toni. It's been a real team effort, and I wanted to say thank you again for trusting me with the added responsibilities of overseeing the interns, and helping to conduct the training for the new clients."

"So much is happening fast. We need all our best players on deck. It's exciting to have all this new business lined up for the new year. That's why the ladies and I agreed on your promotion. We know how much you love the flexibility of the job, and we want you to know we've got your back every step of the way."

Alicia smiled and jabbed the air with her right thumb up. She went back in her office as Toni continued down the corridor. Toni stopped in the break room to get a cup of coffee, and she saw Lorna hunched over her own mug apparently lost in thought. She looked terrible. Toni poured some coffee and sat across the table from Lorna. Lorna failed to make eye contact. She merely said good morning in a dull voice.

"Hey, Lorna, you okay?"

Lorna sat up straight, pushed a strand of hair out of her face, and nodded. "I'm okay. Just feeling a little down in the dumps."

"Why? What's wrong?"

"Charles is getting out of jail."

Toni's heart sank. She knew Lorna felt secure knowing her assailant was behind bars. She also knew Charles would get out eventually. She just didn't think it would be so soon.

"You sure about that?" Toni asked. "I thought he got sentenced to a year."

"He's out early on good behavior. First-time offender and all that crap. As it turns out, he gets to strangle me in front of witnesses and he still ends up with a stupid slap on the wrist. It really makes me want to throw things!" Lorna said, raising her voice. "I just don't know what I'm gonna do if he starts stalking me again. Maybe I should buy me a Glock."

Toni reached over and patted Lorna's right hand. Ignoring Lorna's comment about buying a semiautomatic pistol, she said, "The restraining order didn't expire. He still can't come anywhere near you without violating the order. And now you can bet dollars to doughnuts he's on parole. If he screws with you in any way, shape, or form, his ass is grass. He'll end up back in the slammer so fast he won't know what hit him. He may be as dumb as a lamp post, but he ain't that dumb. Trust me. He doesn't want a fast track back to lockup."

Toni wasn't so sure, though. If Charles got it into his thick head to come after Lorna, possibly blame her for all his legal hassles, then there was little or nothing anybody could do about it until he made a move. Toni always had felt it was messed up that victims of domestic violence often had a hard time proving their cases in court. She understood how victims might be so worn down they didn't want to act, but, on a deeper emotional level, she also understood why Lorna might want to consider blowing the asshole's head off with a Glock 17 if he came within fifty feet of her. She could tell Lorna was skeptical too. They were all too well aware of how unstable Charles was, and that Lorna was in potential danger with or without the restraining order. Still, there was nothing more Lorna could do, other than perhaps take karate lessons to learn how to defend herself. Or maybe buy that pistol after all.

"I know you're upset," Toni said, standing up from the table with her coffee. "I would be too if I were in your shoes, but you gotta believe everything'll be okay. If you spend every waking hour worrying about what Charles may or may not do next, you'll go bonkers. Absolutely stark raving mad. You know that, don't you?"

Lorna nodded. "I can't stop thinking about the bastard. It's like he's in my head and won't get out."

"You know how I feel about positive and negative self-talk," Toni said.

"How could I not? You talk about it practically every single day. Sometimes I just wish you'd give it a damn rest."

Toni laughed, took a sip of her coffee. "The trick is to tell your mind everything will be fine, and you are in control, not Charles. You're in the power seat."

"Easier said than done," Lorna said. She got up from the table, went to the sink, and poured the rest of her coffee out. She turned around, leaned her butt against the edge of the counter, and said, "You wanna know what sucks the most about all this?"

Toni put her coffee mug on the counter. "What?" she asked.

"After all this shit … I still love the asshole. Can you believe that?"

Toni certainly could. She nodded and said, "You don't have to explain things to me. You know I've been there. But you can't be with someone who has all these issues just so you won't have to be alone. Like all of us, you have to stand on your own two feet and not let a man define who you are. You have to define who you are. Nobody else, not even your therapist, can do that for you."

Lorna dabbed at her eyes with a napkin. "But what if he does come around? I don't know if I can trust myself to tell him no."

Toni took a deep breath. "You know, Lorna, we often think we're doing the right thing by letting toxic people into our lives as long as we have love, but it's the uncertainty of love that's so frightening. Now you're gonna have to put that ugly part of your life behind you, and go on without shame and worry." She paused for a moment, and then continued. "You may think you're different, but you're just like me and Audrey and every other female out there. We have to remain strong and don't treat this like it's the only chance of love we'll ever have, because it's not. The good news is there are still some good men in the world. Plenty of fish in the sea, as they say. You need to stop and take time out for yourself. Right now. You can always go fishing later."

"I guess you're right, Toni. Because underneath all this pain I still want another chance at love. I truly don't want to be a victim anymore."

Toni gave Lorna a hug. "You are not a victim. I've always known you to be a survivor. Keep telling yourself that. Remember the positive—"

Lorna held up both hands, palms facing Toni, and said, "Self-talk. Yeah, yeah, yeah. I get it. You've told me a zillion time."

"Sometimes repeating the message is what it takes to close a sale."

"Sometimes beating a dead horse is just plain tiring," Lorna said.

"Uh-huh. You may be right about that."

Toni released her hold and looked Lorna squarely in the eyes. "But, say it out loud. I am not a victim. I am a survivor."

Lorna swallowed hard. Her lips quivered as she tried to respond. "I … I am not a victim. *I am a survivor!*"

"There you go! No one deserves to be abused. Now that you've reclaimed your power, come on! Let's go get this team meeting started. I'm sure Audrey and Alicia are waiting for us in the conference room."

Toni interlocked her arm with Lorna's and they walked down the hall together. The door to the conference room was open, and on the table was a bowl of fruits, bottled waters, and notepads and pens. Audrey and Alicia weren't there yet, but Toni recognized the two young ladies who were seated at the conference table, both of whom were about nineteen years of age. Alicia had hired these two interns to help carry the additional workload that resulted from the publicity the agency was getting.

"Good morning, Lisa and Jackie," Toni said.

Both ladies stood up to shake hands and almost simultaneously said, "Good morning, Ms. Summers."

"Oh," Toni laughed, "no need to be so formal. But I do appreciate it, though. Have a seat. We'll get started as soon as Audrey and Alicia arrive."

Audrey ran her right hand through her fiery red dreadlocks. She exhaled loudly and shook her head, almost as if she was trying to wake herself up after lapsing into a heavy sleep. It had been a terribly hectic day. The new interns were creative and fun, but working with them was akin to herding cats. The young ladies had opinions about everything, and they weren't afraid to share them. Audrey smiled knowingly as she recognized a version of her younger self in the interns.

"I guess we all gotta start somewhere," she mumbled.

Yawning and stretching, Audrey leaned back in her chair and looked up at the ceiling just as the phone on her desk rang. She saw the caller was using her private line, a number few people possessed. Frowning, she didn't recognize the caller ID. She hesitated, wondering if she should bother to pick up or not.

"Oh, hell," she said, picking up the receiver and hitting the button to connect with the caller. "Audrey Simmons speaking."

The voice on the other end of the line was male, cheery, and pleasant. She grinned when the man identified himself as Barry.

"You know!" he said with a laugh. "I'm Steve's friend. From the club. You can't have forgotten singing your guts out at karaoke with you and your girlfriend … uh, colleague from work."

Audrey laughed, picturing Toni and her onstage like some all-girl high-school duo singing their guts out to a crowd of mostly drunk partiers. Barry and Steve had joined them about halfway through the evening, and they truly did have a wonderful time together. It was as if all the troubles of the world had vanished for several blissful hours. She recalled just how smitten Barry seemed to have been with her during the course of the evening, and while she'd been ambivalent about David, still was, in fact, Barry's undivided attention to her had instilled a sense of self-confidence she'd been lacking of late. In short, Barry was like a breath of fresh air.

"Oh, how could I forget?" Audrey said. "I'm so embarrassed. We all got a little out of hand, as I recall."

Barry laughed. "No problem. A girl's gotta let her hair down every once in a while, right?"

"That's right. You know what they say. All work and no play make Jane a bore."

"I don't think that's quite how the saying goes," Barry laughed.

"But - you get my drift."

"I do." Barry paused. "I was hoping you might be free for dinner this Friday. I really enjoyed meeting you, and I'd like to get to know you better."

Audrey cringed. The last thing she wanted was to jump into another fledgling relationship. And yet another part of her was flattered and pleased about the attention she was getting. It did indeed make her feel special.

"I'm not sure, Barry. I did tell you I'm coming off a recent breakup. So, I'm naturally a bit gun shy about jumping back into the deep end of the pool again. You can understand that, I'm sure."

"I definitely understand. If you'd like, we can get together another time," Barry said. "I just wanted to touch base with you. You've been on my mind, and I just wanted you to know that."

This stunned Audrey. The fact he'd accommodate her without making a fuss struck her as intriguing and unusual. She thought back to that night she and Toni went out on the town, that famous karaoke blitz had gotten Barry and his friend's attention. One of the things she'd liked about Barry was his sensitivity and great sense of humor. She didn't mind his good looks either.

Oh, hell, she thought. *You only live once.*

"Uh, no," she said. "Let's do this. I think it might be good for me to get out and about. Lots has been going on at work … all good, but super busy. So, sure. Where and what time?"

24

Toni pulled her winter jacket close up under her chin to protect against the chilly December wind blowing through the semi-bare branches of the deciduous trees encircling the confines of Charlie Loudermilk Park in Buckhead Village. She paused, hands thrust into her pockets against the cold, and let out a deep breath, causing a brief puff of gray vapor before the breeze dissipated it. She looked across the road toward the Buckhead Theater, a place she had sometimes frequented with Donovan, and she immediately felt sad and angry at the same time as she pictured them together in happier days.

Why, she wondered, was she apparently always right when it came to men after the relationship went south, but never beforehand? She went into relationships with the optimism of youth, believing with all her heart every time things would suddenly be different, only to come out on the other side with the cynicism and bitterness of a hag. She wasn't sure if she should just bow out of all things male and start raising cats, but the thought did poke its way to the forefront of her mind more and more often. The coming holidays didn't help. She dreaded them.

The dating scene in the new century was totally alien to her, what with the online aspect taking such a hold over love and seemingly everything else in daily life. The internet was everywhere. Cell phones were becoming human appendages. Nobody liked to talk anymore. They texted instead. As the technology increased connectivity, Toni was all too well aware it was putting distance between people that hadn't existed in the same way prior to the digital millennium. The buzz and hum followed by, "You've got mail!" The march of progress was unstoppable, but Toni wondered if that march was toward a society that increasingly marked its territory with technological and financial divides, which separated communities instead of bringing them together.

At the ripe old age of thirty-five, soon to be thirty-six in January, Toni felt used up and worn out in terms of her search for love. Donovan was now history. They'd tried to keep the relationship intact. They'd both tried very hard to preserve the love that had grown up and flourished earlier in the year. Ultimately, the love wasn't strong enough to go the distance, and that made Toni feel angry and foolish … as if Donovan had played her even as she knew he had not. The reality of the situation was neither party could be entirely to blame for the demise of what had once seemed like the real deal, a once-in-a-lifetime love that could never break.

Well, so much for that relationship, she thought.

Toni sighed. She shook her head, as if to throw off her depression, and she continued her walk along the chic streets of upscale Buckhead Village. High-rise condos and office buildings created a scenic cityscape, one that pleased Toni. She liked to people watch as she walked, and she soon found herself in one of the many tree-lined residential neighborhoods replete with single-family homes, white picket fences, and kids shooting hoops in driveways. She felt a pang of envy. She'd always wanted a nice house in the burbs, kids, probably a Pomeranian dog, and she feared she never would have any of those things because she was too busy to find the right guy to share her life with. She was also too self-protective, and that tendency to withdraw into her shell of assertive authority drove men away.

Christmas music piped out to the street from the shops made her feel even more alone and depressed. She paused in front of a window that showed a nativity scene with all the usual suspects, including the donkey. Her aunt, Gloria had so loved the Christmas holidays. Toni remembered that about her even though she'd died when Toni was just five years old. She remembered decorating the Christmas tree, baking cookies, and watching *Frosty the Snowman* cartoons on TV. She, like her aunt, also loved Christmas. She insisted on buying a live tree, despite the hassle of dropped needles, in part because it brought back the childhood memories, she held dear. She luxuriated in the fresh scent of pine in the great room of her condo, and she usually got a tremendous amount of joy in the simple act of decorating the tree.

"Do I buy a tree this year or not?" she whispered.

She was already late in the Summers' family Christmas tradition. The tree typically went up right after Thanksgiving, and now here it was almost Christmas Eve and she hadn't put up a single holiday decoration … not one fake Santa, reindeer, elf, or candy cane. It struck her as perversely funny the pain she felt over the dissolution of her relationship with Donovan reared up more intensely in the holidays. She succeeded in burying her head in the proverbial sand while throwing herself into her work, but she couldn't run away from herself in those quiet hours when the phones were silent and the computers were turned off. In those moments, she had to face up to the fact she might never find love, she might always go through life alone, and she might die that way too.

In an attempt to shake off the blues, Toni went into a local bar and sat down. She ordered a strawberry martini, and nursed it after the bartender set the glass and the shaker down in front of her.

"Looks like we might actually get some snow," he said, nodding toward the front window. "Sure feels like it. You know … it's like in the air or something. You know that smell? The snow smell?"

Toni shot him a wan smile. People incessantly talked about the weather, and they almost always complained about it.

"Snow smell?" she asked. "That's a good one."

The bartender laughed. "I know. Right? But you know what I mean, don't you?"

Toni did, and she said so. He was right. The smell of winter was in the air. While she wouldn't smell woodsmoke from fireplaces in her upscale urban neighborhood, she imagined it. She pictured snow-draped pines, the swirl of gray-blue smoke drifting lazily up from the chimney, and she could almost smell the homey scent of coffee and hot cinnamon buns.

"Mountains'll probably get slammed," Toni said. "Not so sure about the city, though."

The bartender, a big white guy with a nice smile, grinned as he wiped down the top of the bar. "Mountains always get the worst of it. That's why I live here, not way up there in the boonies."

"I hear ya," Toni said.

"I've seen you around. You live in the area?" the bartender asked.

Toni nodded. "Yeah, not far from here."

"You stayin' around for the holidays? Or headin' out to see family?"

Toni ordinarily didn't like it when strangers engaged her in uninvited conversations, but she found herself warming up to the bartender. He exuded good cheer, and she needed that. She thought perhaps it might rub off on her by osmosis. She made the conscious choice to be positive.

"Not really sure," she said. "I may go down to Savannah to visit my sister and her family. Got a lot of work, though. Not sure what I'm gonna do."

"Oh, come on! Family is always first in my book! Don't let work get in the way of what's really important. Not at this time of year!"

"That's often easier said than done," Toni said. "Putting family first. Besides, some families dredge up old ghosts that should stay buried under five tons of concrete."

The bartender laughed. "I know what you mean about ghosts. You wouldn't believe the stuff I hear during the holidays when people are really sloshed and looking back on their lives with nothing but regret. I just try to let people know there's always room to be sad at another time. Just like there's always time to be poor. The holidays are for joy! They're for us to celebrate each other. They're for us to celebrate Jesus! You know what I mean?"

Toni laughed, and shook her head. "Praise the Lord!"

"Uh-huh! And how!" he said. "You want another strawberry martini?"

"Don't mind if I do," Toni said, pushing her empty glass toward the bartender."

"Sure thing!" he said. "Comin' right up!"

The bartender mixed her drink, and then moved on down the bar to serve another customer. She nursed her second martini as she listened to Christina Aguilera croon a cover of the 1940s Christmas hit song, "Have Yourself a Merry Little Christmas." She smiled as she recalled her recent trip two weeks ago, to the Blue Ridge Mountains with Audrey and Lorna. She'd called it their new millennium mountain retreat, a corporate teambuilding adventure that really served as an excuse for an all-girls vacation to recharge their batteries before the big push to come in the new year. Thanks to Toni's business-to-business marketing plan, the new accounts development arm of the company continued to produce impressive results, and the future looked bright for all three of them if they kept up the good work.

The three-bedroom cabin they'd rented was a rustic beauty. It featured floor-to-ceiling panoramic windows, a well-equipped kitchen, and a wraparound porch. Several Adirondack chairs and a coffee table were situated on the porch, affording exquisite views of the beautiful mountains. There was also an outdoor gas grill, a spacious hot tub, and a firepit. Off to the side of the cabin was an enormous pile of stacked firewood. They spent the long weekend mostly relaxing, which was the whole point of the retreat.

Toni particularly enjoyed the day-long pampering session at a wellness spa, as did Audrey and Lorna. They'd gone for the works—a steam sauna, a Swedish massage, and a cleansing facial. Afterward, she and her friends drank champagne from fluted glasses while they got their manicures and pedicures. The trip represented a welcome diversion from the press of business, and from the turmoil that marked Toni's personal life for much of the year. Since her two friends also faced some friction in their relationships with men, they all agreed to stay out of the dating game for a while.

And then Audrey gave in when Barry called to ask her out on a date. She claimed it wasn't serious, just more of a formal meet and greet, as opposed to the craziness in the karaoke room. She said she liked the guy, and she might let him into her life after he mustered out of the navy subsequent to his next six-month deployment aboard a guided missile cruiser.

As Toni sat at the bar looking back on the year that had nearly passed, she wondered about why it was people couldn't seem to go through life without searching for a companion to share their experiences with. To her mind, especially after her difficult childhood, people were born alone, and they died alone. They deluded themselves into thinking another person in one's life could change that, but she knew the notion was untrue. A companion, a soul mate, merely made the lonely journey more bearable. The fact that Audrey accepted Barry's invitation didn't surprise Toni, not when she really thought about the reason why.

She had no doubt Lorna would eventually go back on the love hunt as well, although Toni wondered if she'd jump back in as easily as Audrey did. At least the trouble with Charles was over, and for that Toni was grateful. They later learned the jerk had moved to New Orleans to live with his sister. He'd stopped trying to contact Lorna shortly after his release from prison, probably thinking better of tempting fate and ending up back inside a cellblock.

For Toni's part in the online dating saga, Donovan had seemed so right for her, a nearly perfect match. He was smart, funny, sensitive, loving, and kind. He never made her feel diminished in any way. He always built her up, encouraged her, and made her feel protected and important. All that was essential to her, and few men had ever delivered the whole package before. Yet the relationship slowly deteriorated after his move to California, and nothing either of them did could deny the fact they were both unwilling to sacrifice their careers for love. Both of them valued the upwardly mobile climb to power, money, and success more than they valued the return on investment love could offer under the right circumstances. When Donovan took his dream job in Silicon Valley, he had done so knowing his relationship with Toni might end. Likewise, when she dismissed the idea of opening an office on the West Coast, she had pretty much done the same thing.

Toni wiped a lone tear from her eye, and drank the rest of her martini. The hard realities of a successful businesswoman were tradeoffs had to be made in order to truly get ahead. She resented the fact most men didn't have to make as many sacrifices, but she also told herself not to dwell on the negative. The positive for the year 2000 was her business had finally taken off in a big way, and it was poised for accelerated growth in 2001.

"Come on, it can't be that bad," the bartender said, yanking her out of her thoughts.

"What?" she asked.

"You look like your dog just died. Cheer up! It's Christmastime! Ho, ho, ho! Merry Christmas!"

"You're too much. I was just thinking about things is all," she said. She held up her empty glass. "Another, please."

The bartender shot her a big smile and set about mixing her drink.

25

Toni glanced at her watch, noting that it was close to nine o'clock as she and Audrey greeted the guests arriving at the entrance to the main ballroom of the Westin Peachtree Plaza hotel. An expansive display of deep red roses stood off to the side, and a string quartet played classical music. The ambiance was subdued at the moment, with only the low hum of conversation. There was no need to shout above the crowd and the music. Soon, the New Year's Eve party would start in earnest, and she looked forward to the fun as well as the exposure the event would give the agency. She'd teamed up with the attorneys upstairs to throw a big party with joint guest lists, making the bash one of the hottest in the city.

Toni greeted an important venture capitalist and his wife, wishing them a happy new year in 2001. "Go on in now," she said, "and enjoy the evening's festivities!"

Toni was dressed to the nines, as were Audrey and Lorna. Toni chose a long-flowing, A-line, spaghetti strap, navy blue silk dress. She matched it with blue silk shoes, a pair of teardrop diamond earrings, and a diamond tennis bracelet.

"People pulled out all the stops in the wardrobe department," Audrey said. "Would you check this out or what!"

Limo after limo pulled up at the entrance, and the passengers exited in full chic and sophisticated attire while others perhaps were a bit over the top. There was plenty of glitter, velvet, deep reds, dark hues, bow ties, leather, and evening gowns with long slits to reveal slender legs.

"I know," Toni said. "I have high hopes for tonight. This event could put us even more on the map."

"From your lips to God's ears."

"Did I tell you that you look marvelous tonight?" Toni asked, drawing out the "marvelous" to tease.

"Why, no, Miss Toni. You did not. Not bad, eh?"

Audrey adjusted the top of her black fitted strapless gown. Then she spun around slowly on her black strappy heels, being careful not to mess up her top bun. The diamonds adorning her hoop earrings, heart-shaped necklace, and tennis bracelet glittered in the lights.

"Not bad at all, Audrey! You look great."

They greeted additional clients, guests, and acquaintances. A few seconds later, Lorna approached them in a short red-sequin wrapped dress that exposed her legs and curvaceous figure. She had paired the dress with a matching red-sequin shoulder bag and shoes.

Lorna put her hand on Toni's shoulder. "Are you ready for tonight? Are we all ready for tonight?"

Toni nodded. "More than ready."

"Well, let's hope everything goes off without a hitch," Audrey said.

"Why don't you ladies take a break. I could stand here and look cute greeting the guests for a while."

"That's a good idea. I do need to check on some things," Toni said.

"Yeah, and I need to go to the ladies' room," Audrey replied.

Audrey grabbed Toni by the arm and they headed inside as if they were each other's date. Toni was pleased at how well the caterers and the hotel had worked together to decorate the ballroom. She especially liked the strands of white helium bubble balloons that covered the entire ceiling. The room was divided into two large areas. A full bar was situated in the center with a huge arrangement of white roses, blue hydrangeas, gardenias, and blue irises.

"God, these flower arrangements are something else," Toni said, leaning over to whisper in Audrey's ear as they walked. "I know we picked the arrangement from online photos, but in real life the colors just take your breath away."

"I know. Just awesome," Audrey said. "See you on the floor doing the mingle. Meanwhile, I gotta go tinkle."

Toni fake punched Audrey's right shoulder. "You best run to it, then," she said with a laugh as she watched her friend hurry away.

Toni surveyed the round tables covered with black-and-white tablecloths, and surrounded by black high-back chairs. A long, narrow buffet table filled with an assortment of appetizers lined one wall. Atop it sat a large ice sculpture of an eagle. The dance floor occupied the rear of the ballroom, where the DJ booth was set up. A disco ball spun above the darkened room, and everything reflected in the mirrors on the surrounding walls.

Knowing that image was everything in PR, Toni was confident she and her team had pulled off a win. She didn't want to count her chickens just yet, though. She knew from long experience that Murphy's Law could spring up at any time. It was never wise to tempt fate by assuming life would refrain from interfering with one's best-laid plans. As she turned to take another pass along the floor to greet and mingle, Audrey hurried up to her.

"Hey, guess who's here already!" Audrey said.

"Who?"

"Scotty! And he looks like a million friggin' bucks in that tux of his."

Toni felt her stomach lurch, as if she was in a panic. The feeling lasted only a few seconds, but it was long enough for her to be aware of it. Scotty and she had been flirting together for years, and nothing had ever come of it because she wasn't interested. And, when she was ready to dip her toe back into the dating pool, she'd found Donovan online and had fallen in love with him. In short, her relationship with Scotty was what it was, and it wasn't likely, in her opinion, to ever amount to anything more than a friendly flirt every now and then.

"He usually does," Toni said, scoping out the room and seeing Scotty heading toward them. "Look like a million bucks, I mean."

Audrey made the sound of a drumroll. "And here comes Atlanta's most eligible bachelor," Audrey said. "Mr. Scotty Walker!"

"Get a grip, girl. You'd think you'd never met the guy before."

Scotty beamed as he stopped in front of them. Toni noticed his attention remained solely on her, though he did smile at Audrey.

"You both look stunning tonight," he said.

He executed an exaggerated bow, sweeping his right arm out in front of him. "Scotty Walker ... at your service, my lady."

He took Toni's right hand in his and gave the top a little kiss.

Toni felt herself blush, and it embarrassed her to think Scotty might have noticed.

"Give it a break, Scotty," Toni said.

Scotty laughed. His laugh was from the soul. She'd always liked his laugh.

"Your wish is my command," he said.

Toni rolled her eyes.

"How much you had to drink already?" Audrey asked. "Save some room for dinner."

"Oh, I'll save plenty of room. Don't you worry about that." Scotty hesitated. Then his face got serious. "You here stag tonight?" he asked.

Toni didn't like the personal nature of the question. It was none of his business if she'd brought a date to the party or not. Still, it was innocent enough, on the face of it. "It's just me tonight."

"Where's your boyfriend? Donovan? Was that his name?"

Toni sighed. "If you must know, Donovan and I haven't been together for months. Things just didn't work out between us after he moved to California to take his dream job."

"Oh, I'm so sorry to hear that," Scotty said. "I didn't know. Otherwise, I wouldn't have asked."

Toni noted the sincerity in his voice. "It's okay, Scotty. No harm. Look, I gotta go check on a few things."

As Toni turned to leave, Scotty gently grabbed her arm, and said, "Save the last dance of the night for me, okay? It would mean a lot if you did."

Scotty's request startled her, and she wasn't sure why. A waiter passed with a tray of glasses full of champagne. Toni reached for a glass and took a sip of her drink. "No promises, but we'll see," she said, looking him intently in the eye.

"That's all a man could ask for," he said.

Toni turned away and headed to the kitchen to check on the operation. Audrey remained by her side.

"So, what's going on here?" Audrey asked.

"What? With Scotty?"

Audrey nodded. "Yeah, with Scotty. Who'd you think I was talkin' about?"

"Nothing." Toni shrugged. "Nothing's going on."

"Doesn't look like nothing."

"Well, it's nothing. Now, you go greet and mingle. I'm gonna check on things in the kitchen, and then I'll join you and Lorna on the mingle patrol."

After seeing all was well with the caterers, Toni roamed the room, meeting, greeting, and taking pictures with the guests. She observed an array of couples and groups immersed in lively conversations, and it pleased her that clearly everyone was having fun. The champagne flowed, and soon the cocktail hour ended and dinner was served. The noise level in the room dropped significantly as everyone ate their meals. The house salad was superb. There were entre options of baked salmon, grilled chicken breast, and prime rib, which was served with a choice of baked potato, garlic mashed potatoes, or rice pilaf and seasonal vegetables. Dessert choices included miniature cheesecakes, cookies, puddings, ice creams, and baked Alaska.

Toni felt a warm hand on her shoulder. She turned to face Lorna with a champagne flute in her hand. "Wow! I told you it was going to be awesome," Lorna said, taking a sip of her champagne. "There are so many cute men here with no wedding rings on. And, guess what, I'm single. So, I'm going to mingle."

"You go for it!" Toni laughed. "Have fun. You deserve it. And don't worry about a thing. I got your back for the evening."

"Okay," she said as she twirled away.

The time flew by in a delightful blur. Glancing around, Toni spotted Theo and Ron, the cohosts of the party, sitting at the bar. She smiled brightly as she joined them. "Happy New Year, guys! You have no idea how happy I am we decided to stage this event together. Between all our respective clients we've got a terrific networking opportunity in addition to having a great time!"

Theo, the elder of the two partners, stood up with a drink in his hand. He cut a powerful figure at over six feet tall with the shoulders of a quarterback. He wore a black long-tailed tuxedo, black cummerbund, white frilled shirt, and matching black bow tie. His salt and pepper hair and beard matched his outfit nicely. He placed his glass on the bar, and opened his arms to greet her. She stepped into his embrace.

"You look fantastic, Toni!" Theo said, releasing her from his hug. "Everything looks great. You guys did a super job putting all this together."

Ron also stood up and greeted her. He was tall at just over six feet, light-skinned, and slender. Toni noted that both attorneys looked as if they had just stepped out of *GQ* magazine.

"What a great way to start off the new year," Ron said. "Looks like we've got tons of the gossip press here. No doubt some of us are going to end up in the spotlight, but in a good way, I hope."

"Yeah … fingers crossed," Toni said. "I think we should get the speeches over with before everyone gets too liquored up."

Both men agreed.

Theo escorted Toni over to the DJ booth, and waited for the last song to finish playing. Taking the microphone, he asked for everyone's attention, and then he invited his and Toni's associates to come up to the stage.

"Good evening, ladies and gentlemen, and welcome," he began. "I'm Theo Warren and this is Toni Summers. On behalf of Toni Summers and Associates, and Warren, Harris, and Daniels, LLC, we want to thank you all for joining us on this festive last night of the year. It is in this time of gratitude that we want to let you know we value your patronage and appreciate each and every one of you for your confidence in us throughout the years. Having you among our clientele is something for which we are deeply indebted. We appreciate your business, and look forward to taking care of all your needs in the future."

Then Theo handed the microphone to Toni. She smiled at the crowd. She'd done lots of public speaking in the past, and she was comfortable with it. Standing onstage and peering out at the crowd, she felt a tremendous sense of accomplishment. Five years earlier, she'd left a dead-end marketing job at an ad agency to cofound the business with her two friends. Now, it seemed like they had truly arrived in the limelight. Clients were pouring in so fast she thought she might need to rent additional office space. She certainly was bringing on more people to meet the workload.

"I'd like to thank you all for coming tonight. We know you could've attended another ball or function to ring in the New Year, but we are most appreciative that you chose to spend the evening with us. Thank you for the pleasure of continuing to work with you. And, on behalf of our entire staff, we want to wish everyone health and prosperity in the new year ahead. Please, enjoy the rest of the evening. It's time to hit the dance floor!"

The crowd cheered when Toni handed the microphone back to the DJ. As she stepped aside, she felt someone tug on her right arm. She turned around and saw Scotty.

"Hey," he said. "Nice speech."

Toni laughed. She patted him on the arm. "Nice of you to say so, but it was nothing really."

"You havin' a good time?" he asked.

"I sure am!" she said.

"Come on. Let's bust a move," he said, taking her hand. "I know it's not the last dance, but what the hell."

Toni laughed again, not believing what he'd just said. "Did you just say bust a move? You can't be serious! Nobody says that anymore."

"Guess I'm showing my age."

"You sure are, you old man, you!"

"Hey, I only just turned forty-one."

"And I forgot your birthday," she said. "Please forgive me," she teased. "I didn't even get you a card." She now had to yell above the music. The party was really starting to rock, and she felt a giddy pleasure in it all.

As Scotty maneuvered them onto the dance floor, he placed his hand on the small of her back to guide her. The DJ spun a balanced mix of tunes to suit most tastes, everything from jazz, to swing, rock, and disco. The floor shook as everyone danced and got into the party. Toni noticed her friends boogying down with two of the junior lawyers on the far side of the room. They waved at her and she waved back. She danced a tune or two more, and then she took Scotty by the hand and said in a voice loud enough for him to hear her.

"Let's get a drink! I sure could use one after all this exercise! I feel like I'm sweating buckets."

Scotty grinned at her. "That sounds like a good idea!"

As they made their way off the dance floor, the DJ played a slow song, Marvin Gaye's "Let's Get It On."

Scotty turned to Toni and said, "It's a slow song. Do you want to wait on that drink for one more dance?"

Toni knew what a slow dance meant. It was one thing to sweat and bop to fast songs. But a slow song meant a romantic jaunt on the dance floor with all the other lovers. She'd been aware the guest list included mostly couples. That was normal. She gazed up at Scotty, who was smiling quizzically down at her. His hazel eyes held hers in a long mutually intense gaze, one she knew she could get lost in forever if she allowed herself to.

"Okay," she said, getting up on her tiptoes to speak into his ear as the song cued up and couples embraced as they moved about the dance floor.

Pulling her close, he slid his arm around her lower back and she rested her head against his chest. For some reason, it felt natural to be in his arms. They'd never slow danced before. Indeed, they'd never danced together at all until then. This was all new to Toni, and she rather liked the way she was feeling. Perhaps she'd had too much champagne. Funny, she wasn't feeling tipsy. She lost herself in the music, in Scotty's scent of part cologne and part sweat from the dancing. He pulled her a little tighter into his embrace. Toni took a deep breath as she closed her eyes.

The slow dance ended at just before midnight. The DJ called the countdown as she stood with Scotty at her side. He reached over and squeezed her hand.

"May this be the best year for you yet," he said, leaning close to speak over the crowd noise.

Holding a fluted glass of champagne in her left hand, she didn't pull away from Scotty with her right hand. She let him hold her hand, as if it was the most natural thing in the world.

"Three ... two ... one!" the DJ shouted. "Happy New Year, everyone!"

Toni clinked glasses with Scotty, and then joined the crowd as they all sang "Auld Lang Syne."

Scotty put his arm around her. "May I?" he asked, holding her close.

"What?" she asked.

"May I kiss you, Miss Toni Summers? For the new year?"

Toni's head told her to back off, the last thing she wanted was to let another man in her life when the business was taking off like a rocket ship. She needed to focus all her attention on work, on bottom-line revenue, and on growing the company into something truly impressive. Yet her body told her something else. She glanced over at Audrey and Lorna laughing with the two junior attorneys at the bar. They seemed to be lost in the moment, almost as lost in it as she was. She gazed up at Scotty and nodded.

Scotty smiled as he tilted her chin upwards, holding it firm to keep her face steady. He leaned down and kissed her gently. Losing herself in him, she put her champagne glass down on the table and hugged him tenderly, luxuriating in the feelings of arousal she had been resisting for so long.

When they parted, her head told her she'd just made a big mistake, she should warn Scotty right then and there the kiss was not a harbinger of a relationship to come. It was just a thing of the moment, a New Year's kiss, and nothing more. Her heart told her to hang on, just for a little longer before reality set in. She didn't know whether her head or her heart would win out in the end. She just knew everything would work out, or it wouldn't.

Toni leaned in closer, put her arms around his neck, and kissed him passionately. Then she stepped back. "Happy New Year, Scotty. I think the year 2001 is going to be interesting. Very interesting!"

Printed in the United States
By Bookmasters